"Tell me if this is going to be a ravishment,"

Bea said. "I need to powder my nose."

"It's not your nose I'm worried about. It's your damaged toe," Russ said, taking off her shoe.

"You're worried?"

"If anything happens to you, I won't get paid for driving you home."

"You're mercenary right to the cockles of your cold heart."

"Guilty."

"I thought ravishments usually started with the blouse."

She gave him a look that would have melted a suit of armor—a deliciously sexy look. *Ravishment.* She had used the word. He was amazed to realize that on the deserted mountain road in the tight confines of his pickup truck, the idea of ravishing her didn't sound so absurd. To feel her yielding body under his. To press his lips against the fluttering pulse point of her throat . . .

"I wouldn't want anything to happen to you, Tiger Lady. Life's more interesting when you're around. . . ."

Dear Reader,

Welcome to Silhouette Romance—experience the magic of the wonderful world where two people fall in love. Meet heroines who will make you cheer for their happiness, and heroes (be they the boy next door or a handsome, mysterious stranger) who will win your heart. Silhouette Romance novels reflect the magic of love—sweeping you away with books that will make you laugh and cry, heartwarming, poignant stories that will move you time and time again.

In the next few months, we're publishing romances by many of your all-time favorites such as Diana Palmer, Brittany Young, Annette Broadrick and many others. Your response to these authors and other authors in Silhouette Romance has served as a touchstone for us, and we're pleased to bring you more books with Silhouette's distinctive medley of charm, wit and—above all—*romance*.

During 1991, we have many special events planned. Don't miss our WRITTEN IN THE STARS series. Each month in 1991, we're proud to present readers with a book that focuses on the hero—and his astrological sign.

I hope you'll enjoy this book and all of the stories to come. Come home to romance—Silhouette Romance—for always!

Sincerely,

Tara Gavin
Senior Editor

PEGGY WEBB

Tiger Lady

Silhouette *Romance*
Published by Silhouette Books New York
America's Publisher of Contemporary Romance

SILHOUETTE BOOKS
300 E. 42nd St., New York, N.Y. 10017

TIGER LADY

Copyright © 1991 by Peggy Webb

ISBN: 0-373-08785-3

First Silhouette Books printing April 1991

Books by Peggy Webb

Silhouette Romance

When Joanna Smiles #645
A Gift for Tenderness #681
Harvey's Missing #712
Venus de Molly #735
Tiger Lady #785

PEGGY WEBB

grew up in a large northeastern Mississippi family in which the southern tradition of storytelling was elevated to an art. "In our family, there was always a romance or a divorce or a scandal going on," she says, "and always someone willing to tell it. By the time I was thirteen, I knew I would be a writer."

Over the years, Peggy has raised her two children—and twenty-five dogs. "Any old stray is welcome," she acknowledges. "My house is known as Dog Heaven." Recently, her penchant for trying new things led her to take karate lessons. Although she was the oldest person in her class and one of only two women, she now has a blue belt in Tansai Karate. Her karate hobby came to a halt, though, when wrens built a nest in her punching bag. "I decided to take up bird-watching," says Peggy.

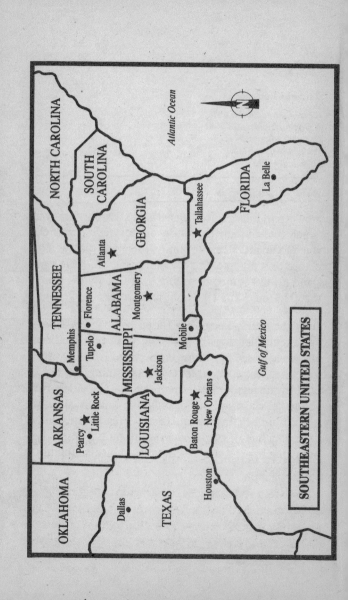

SOUTHEASTERN UNITED STATES

Chapter One

She was going home.

Except for the purple shadows cast across the road by the Quachita Mountains, Beatrice Adams didn't notice her surroundings. She was thinking ahead, seeing exactly how her mother would look, her hair mostly gray now, cropped short and flying untamed and tousled around her smiling face.

Glory Ethel never lost her smile. That's what Bea remembered most about her mother. Even in the lean years after her husband had left her with two small children to raise, Glory Ethel had kept her brave and beautiful smile.

She was a rock, and Bea was headed for the security of her mother. Having just come off another disastrous relationship, Bea needed Glory Ethel to hug her and say, "Everything will work out all right, honey, just you wait and see."

Of course, Bea knew that everything wouldn't work out all right simply because her mother said so, but it made her feel better to hear the words. It gave her hope, however faint, that someday, somewhere, she would meet a man she wouldn't be afraid to love, a man she wouldn't automatically expect to get up at the first hint of trouble and walk out the door—just the way her father had done so many years ago.

The tape she had been listening to ran out. She reached over, took it out, then popped a Billie Holliday tape in. She did everything by feel, for she had organized her tapes before she left Dallas, and she knew Billie Holliday was next after the Grover Washington, Jr. jazz tape.

That's the way she was, organized about everything—even to the way she selected men. She never dated any except the suitable ones, the ones with manners and good jobs and lots of potential; and then, little by little she began to pick them to pieces in her mind, finding fault until they couldn't do anything right. They all ended up walking out the door. Some literally, and some just sending farewell notes or leaving messages on her machine.

Her friend Margaret, who was a psychologist and trained to know about such things, said Bea deliberately drove men away before any serious relationships developed so she wouldn't risk abandonment later, after the love had started, when it would hurt the most. Maybe Margaret was right. Bea didn't know.

She sighed. You wouldn't think a grown woman would let something that happened to her when she was thirteen years old stay with her for years and years, especially an educated, sensible, intelligent woman. But that's how it was.

Maybe she'd get over it. Maybe she'd get over her father, Taylor Adams, leaving them. Her brother had.

A smile curved Bea's lips as she thought about seeing her brother again.

Samuel never changed. He would still be as darkly handsome as Clark Gable, and just as full of power and charm. These days, though, he was more mellow. Being married had done that to him. Love had been kind to Samuel. And finally it had been kind to her mother. She had met a wonderful man two years ago, through a lonely hearts column, of all things.

As for Bea . . . just thinking about taking a chance on love gave her ulcers. And headaches.

She wouldn't think about that. She had a good job, good health and a family who loved her—every reason in the world to be happy. Besides that, she was going home.

Tomorrow. She'd be back in Florence, Alabama, this time tomorrow.

As she took her Jaguar smoothly around a mountain curve, she hummed along with the Billie Holliday tape. She was content.

Just around the bend, her Jaguar coughed once and died. Bea was astonished. She'd had the car serviced before she left Dallas, just as she always did before a trip. She didn't understand how the unexpected could be happening to her.

She sat in the car, her humming stilled, her fingers drumming on the steering wheel. Outside, the sun was rapidly dropping behind the mountains. There was a little daylight left, but not much. She switched Billie Holliday off and reached into her car pocket to consult her map. Lured by the promise of mountain craft shops, she had left the main highway about midafternoon.

According to the map, she was on a county road some-where between Caddo Gap and Pearcy, Arkansas. She was about as far from civilization as she could get.

If she had flown home, none of this would be hap-pening. Of course, she might have dropped out of the sky and that would be that. Bea didn't think the skies were friendly. You couldn't pay her enough money to fly.

Sitting on the lonely road with her car refusing to budge, she wished that she was the kind who called her travel agent and booked herself on airplanes going everywhere from Paris, France, to Florence, Alabama; but if wishes were horses beggars would ride, her mother always said.

So Bea stopped her foolish wishing and took action instead. Folding the map shut, she placed it back in the car pocket and took out her owner's manual. Surely there was nothing wrong that a level head and a steady pair of hands couldn't fix.

She released her hood, then got her winter coat from the back seat and stepped outside. The inner workings of a car were a mystery to her. It took ten minutes just to identify the parts. Once she'd done that, she set about trying to find the problem. Unfortunately, a broken car never looked broken. There were no gapping holes or frazzled wires or smoking pipes. There was only the dark, forbidding mystery of a foreign-built engine.

She heard the vehicle coming down the road before she saw it. The driver was either practically deaf or had a perverse penchant for loud noise. Country-and-western music came around the bend two minutes be-fore the truck.

She looked over the hood of her car. The truck was electric blue and very, very old. It rattled with every inch of ground it covered. And it had to be rattling mightily to be heard over the music.

"Hi." The truck had stopped alongside her. Its driver was leaning out the window, smiling. "Need any help?"

Bea quickly assessed him. With his wide smile and his nice blue eyes, he looked friendly and harmless enough, though the thick shock of blond hair and the beard did make him look like a pirate. A person could never be sure about strangers, especially strange men, and especially on lonely mountain roads.

"Everything is under control." Shouting to be heard over the music, she waved her manual at him, wondering at the same time if there would be anybody around to hear her if she screamed. She doubted it. Anyhow, she wasn't the screaming type. If anything needed taking charge of, she took charge, whether it was an ornery car or an ornery man. "I'm sure there's nothing wrong that I can't fix."

"All that beauty and brains, too. How refreshing."

Any kind feelings she'd had about her rescuer died a dramatic death. He was the worst of his breed: an oversized chauvinistic male who expected nothing of women except an empty head. What else could she expect of a man who announced his presence with country music? Hadn't that floozy her father had run off with done the same thing? Sashayed into Florence, twanging her guitar and her hips at the same time, and waltzed off with Taylor Adams and his fortune?

Bea drew herself up to her full height, impressive by any standards, particularly with her high heels, then put on the look that quelled presumptuous male co-workers and deluded Don Juans.

"I'm not standing in the middle of the road to be refreshing. I'm here to repair a car. Will you excuse me?"

She stuck her head under the hood and searched in earnest for something to fix.

The driver turned his obnoxious music down a notch, just low enough so she could hear his wicked chuckle.

"You don't mind if I watch, do you?" Without waiting for an answer, he turned off the engine and climbed down from his truck.

She watched him out of the corner of her eye. He was big, impressively big. And handsome in a rugged, devilish sort of way. Just the kind of flamboyant, shallow man she'd expected.

He leaned against the door of his truck, watching her with an amused expression on his face. Her first instinct was to say something cutting enough to send him on his way; then she thought better of it. Her car might be seriously ailing, and she didn't want to be stranded in the dark. As much as it would pain her to ask him for help, she might have to send him to the nearest phone to call a tow truck.

"I don't like to work with an audience, but you can stay as long as you don't block my light." She nodded toward the sun, slowly sinking westward behind his back.

"Never let it be said that I interfered with the work of a beautiful woman mechanic." He left his truck and came around to the front of her car. "You *are* a mechanic, aren't you?"

"Of course I'm a mechanic. My hands are not only worth a hundred and fifty thousand dollars each, they are also lethal."

"Lethal?"

"Karate. Black belt." She'd lied about being a mechanic—some perverse urge of hers, and she never had perverse urges. She hadn't lied about the martial arts, though.

"I'm impressed."

He didn't look impressed. He still looked as if he had a ringside seat at a circus performed especially for him.

"Then perhaps I should charge admission."

"You have a sense of humor, too. I like that." He leaned closer, peering over her shoulder and getting in her way. "Do you have a name, pretty lady?"

Pretty lady, indeed. As if a woman was nothing more than a glimpse of stocking and a puff of powder.

"I do, but I'm sure men of your type wouldn't bother to use it. Call me Bubbles or Boopsy or whatever it is men like you call pretty ladies." She jiggled a wire that looked suspicious. Nothing happened. "Just don't expect me to answer."

"That's fine by me, Boopsy. I'm just here to watch."

Russ Hammond had never met a woman with such a long stinger. But then, he'd asked for every barb she'd sunk into his flesh. It made life easier—keeping people at a distance. He'd had years and years of practice, and he was an expert at it.

In the fading light, he watched as the woman poked and prodded her car. Every now and then she consulted her owner's manual. Obviously she was not a mechanic. But then, neither was he. If he had known anything at all about cars, he'd have fixed hers and been on his way. All clean and neat and uninvolved. But he had no talent with broken cars. Some latent chivalry—promoted, no doubt, by the spectacular view of setting sun on the majestic mountain—had caused him to stop, and that same misbegotten gallantry made him stay.

He watched as the woman with the shiny black hair and the cool white skin continued her futile efforts. She never appeared frustrated, never looked disgusted, never said a word. She merely looked determined. He decided that's how George Washington must have looked crossing the Delaware.

"Do you mind if I make a suggestion?" he asked, just as the last ray of light disappeared from the sky. She looked up and quirked one eyebrow at him. "Why don't you hop aboard my trusty vehicle here and let me take you into the nearest town? We might still find a garage open."

"I don't want to leave the car."

Translated, that meant, *I don't want to get into a truck with a strange man, particularly that truck and that man.* He didn't have to guess; her face said it all. He might have argued that riding with him was safer than staying on a lonely mountain road in the dark, but he didn't. What was her safety to him?

"Then I'll just mosey on down the road." He started toward his truck, saying over his shoulder, "I'll stop at the nearest town and send a tow truck back for you."

"I'll pay you, of course."

"And ruin a vagabond's honor? No, thank you." He climbed into his truck. Loud music and revving engine crashed into the silence. Leaning out his window, he saluted. "Goodbye, Tiger Lady."

Bea watched as his truck rattled around the bend. When the last flicker of taillights had disappeared, she lowered the hood and climbed back into her Jag, carefully locking all her doors. Chances were good he'd forget her the minute he was out of sight. That's what she wanted—to be forgotten, but not until he'd dispatched a tow truck.

She turned the ignition key so she could listen to the soothing sounds of Billie Holliday. Right in the middle of "Love Me or Leave Me," she heard the man's parting words. *Tiger Lady.* Now where had that come from?

Russ rattled down the road, slowly leaving the woman and her Jaguar behind. *Tiger Lady?* What in the devil had prompted him to call her that? Pet names were for pet people. He's never even had a pet dog that lasted longer than two weeks. What would he do with a pet person?

He put the thought of the woman out of his mind and concentrated on the sharp mountain curves. In all his bumming around, he'd never made it to this part of the country. He didn't know what was around the next bend or even where the nearest town was, for that matter. For the most part, he traveled without the aid of maps. Aimless wandering suited his purpose. Or his lack of purpose.

He didn't keep track of time, either, so it could have been fifteen minutes or forty-five before he came into the small community—Pearcy, the sign read. He drove down the middle of the town. For all the activity, it might have been recently hit by the plague. All the houses were dark, the shops were closed up tight and the town's only garage looked totally abandoned. Just to make certain, he got out of his truck and knocked loudly at the office door. His only answer was the forlorn "meow" of an alley cat passing by.

"Dammit." He pulled the collar of his jacket up against the chill of the evening and started back to his truck. He could drive on to the next town, wherever that might be, and hope to find a garage open. Or he could forget the woman. Somebody else was bound to come along and help her. Anyway, she wasn't his worry.

He opened his truck door and climbed back inside.

Forgetting her would be the best thing all the way around. His decision didn't make him feel good, but hell, he wasn't about to get tangled up with another big-eyed helpless female. Nobility wasn't worth suffering for.

He chuckled to think how angry the woman in the road would be to know he was thinking of her as helpless.

They all were. Till they got what they wanted. Take Lurlene, for instance. His wife down in LaBelle, Florida. Well, she used to be his wife. She wasn't anymore. Not since he'd walked in and found her on their four-poster bed with the B-Quick Man. It was right funny now that it was all over and he could think about it without wanting to take his shotgun and blow them to Kingdom Come.

Wormy little old Horace Clemmens had been thought of as the B-Quick Man because he ran a printing shop in Labelle called by that name. It had taken on new meaning the day Russ had come in from his orange groves and seen old Horace, skinny bottom and all, showing that two-timing Lurlene a trick or two.

And to think he'd once felt sorry for her with her story of having no place to go. He'd even been willing to give up his wandering ways and settle down in a white-washed house and two hundred acres of orange groves. It probably wouldn't sound like much to most folks, but it was more than he had ever had. Lurlene, too.

Thank goodness he'd never been foolish enough to believe he loved her. But it was the closest he'd ever come, and he'd paid the price. He didn't ever want to see LaBelle, Florida, again, as long as he lived.

But that was all behind him now. And so was that woman on the road in her fancy broken-down car. He'd just mosey on out of her life.

His key was in the ignition when he heard the music. He cocked his head, listening. It was drifting his way from both ends of town, "Almost Persuaded" from one side and "Pass Me Not" from the other.

The truth dawned. That's where everybody was, Sunday-night church services. As the words came faintly to him, wafting on the mountain breezes, he smiled. The woman had powerful allies. How could he turn his back on her when guardian angels were urging her rescue?

Shaking his head at his own foolishness, and still grinning, he turned his truck around. He was going back for the tiger lady.

Bea heard the rattle before she saw the truck. She had almost resigned herself to spending the night in the car. Shading her eyes against the glare of approaching headlights, she peered into the darkness. He had come back, her blond rescuer. The wheezing, clanking truck was unmistakably his.

He climbed from his truck and tapped on her window. She eased it down.

"Where's the tow truck?"

"At your service." He waved his arm toward the ramshackle vehicle.

"You must be joking. That truck looks as if it will barely carry you, let alone tow a car."

"I'm afraid its your best bet under the circumstances. The town is locked up tight as a drum. From the looks of things, everybody has gone to church."

"It's Sunday... of course." Bea got out of her car to assess the situation. She walked around his truck, kicking the tires and pressing her weight against the fenders.

"Maybe you'd like to check my chassis, too."

Her rescuer was leaning nonchalantly against the fender of her Jag, the glow in his eyes announcing very plainly that what he did best was have women check his chassis.

"No, thank you." She put all the chill of the October evening in her reply.

"You're not even tempted, I guess."

"Not remotely."

"Good." He unfolded his long legs and began to unload gear from the pickup. "Now that we don't have that to worry about, we can get on with this tow job." He uncoiled a length of chain. "The name's Russ Hammond, and if you want to get into that little burg they call Pearcy before next December, you'd better get a move on, Tiger Lady."

"The name's Bea Adams, and we might as well get one thing clear—I'll do whatever it takes to get into Pearcy save one thing. I will not grovel on my knees in your stunning male presence, nor will I kiss your chauvinistic boots."

He propped one foot on the tailgate of the truck. "So you noticed. Gen-u-ine snakeskin, taken right off the hide of an ornery old python that slithered that way. I'm hell on snakes, ma'am." He grinned. "You sure you won't change your mind about kissing them?"

"Your sense of humor almost redeems you, but not quite. Your sins are far too numerous."

"I try." He handed her a flashlight. "Here. Hold this while I rig up a tow."

The chain rattled and clanked as he began to hook it on to the bumper of the Jaguar.

"You're sure you know what you're doing?" She trained the flashlight on his hands.

"This is not my everyday work, but I'm the best you've got, unless you want to wait until somebody better comes along."

That was true. She'd waited nearly two hours in the dark while he went to summon help, and not one vehicle had passed her way. It was just her luck to be stuck with the most aggravating man west of the Mississippi.

She trained the light closer to his work. "Are you sure those chains will hold?"

"No." He glanced up with a look as cold as the Arctic. "I'm not sure about anything in life. Are you?"

"Only the things I'm in charge of."

Russ turned back to his work. "Are you in charge of much?"

"An advertising firm in Dallas, the *best* in Dallas."

"It figures. You look like the kind who wouldn't associate herself with anything except the best."

The words sounded like a compliment, but the tone sounded like an insult. She didn't know why she even bothered to care. Once she got to Pearcy, or wherever he'd said the next town was, she'd never see him again. Thank goodness.

She watched while Russ eased his pickup in front of her Jaguar and hooked the vehicles together. It was an unlikely pairing.

"All set," he said.

She caught the door handle of her car. He reached out and covered her hand.

"You can't ride back here."

"Of course I can. It's my car."

"Don't be ridiculous."

"I'm never ridiculous." She opened her car door.

"Then don't be so damned stubborn." He slammed the door shut. "Just what kind of ride do you think you'd have, bumping along back here, chained to my truck? And what do you think you'd do if the chain broke loose?"

"Well, it looks like it will hold."

"That's all I need. A bossy, stubborn woman."

"You make me sound like the plague."

"Tiger Lady, you are." He caught her wrist and propelled her toward his truck. The door squeaked on rusty hinges as he opened it. "Get in."

She knew he was right. But she hated being told what to do, especially by a man with his primitive, Me-Tarzan-You-Jane attitude. She favored him with a fierce glare before lifting one foot inside the truck. Her skirt was tight and the truck was far off the ground. In order not to tear the black garbardine, she hoisted her skirt over her knees.

Russ swatted her on the behind and gave her a boost. "In you go, Toots."

"Has anyone ever told you that your kind belongs in the jungle, swinging from vines?"

"Aren't you the lucky one? Tonight's my night off." He got in himself and started the engine. "I was hoping for a nice quiet night with a glass of coconut juice before I had to go back to the jungle. Instead, I got you." Easing the truck into gear, he started down the road.

"I intend to pay you handsomely for your troubles."

"My needs are modest. You can buy the gas."

"Deal."

They drove along, not speaking, for the next five minutes. The only sounds were the rattle-banging of the old truck and bump of tires along the rutted mountain road.

"Do you mind if I listen to music?"

She was surprised he'd asked.

"A little Chopin might be nice."

Grinning, he turned on the radio. A twangy rendition of an old sob song burst forth from the bowels of the truck. It was country-and-western at its worst—and its loudest.

Bea sat stoically and tried not to listen. She'd already let him rile her. What was more, she'd let him *see* that he'd riled her. Never in her life had she lost so much control with a man. She'd endure his music if it killed her—and it just might. Already her stomach was in knots and her throat felt tight. She never heard country-and-western without thinking of her father's betrayal.

"Do you like it?" he yelled.

"Love it." She gave him a Cheshire-cat grin.

He tapped his fingers on the steering wheel in time to the music. Any fool could see she hated his music. Good. The more he ruffled her feathers, the better off he was. He never should have stopped for her in the first place. And he certainly never should have gone back for her.

They'd soon be to Pearcy, though. He'd leave her then, leave her and never look back.

Chapter Two

"*This* is Pearcy?"

Bea could count the buildings of Main Street on one hand—the small red-brick post office, a dilapidated garage that doubled as a service station, Freddy's General Store, and a beauty shop, its painted sign nearly as big as the whitewashed shed that supported it.

"Afraid so."

"Are you sure this is the closest town?"

"Maybe I'm going blind. Did you see another town on this road?"

"There was a turnoff a mile back. It might go somewhere civilized."

"It might go straight to New York City."

Russ turned up his music. Just to aggravate her more, he whistled along. Whistling was a special talent of his. Not only could he carry the tune, he could whistle louder than any other kid in the fifth grade. That's when he'd learned.

He looked at her out of the corner of his eye to see how she was taking it. Poorly, judging by the way her nose pinched in and her mouth pursed together.

He'd be rid of her soon. He slowed his truck, peering around for somebody, anybody, to take charge of Bea Adams. There was not a soul in sight. Nor was there a sound. Apparently everybody had gone home from church, just vanished into the hills and hollows of the Quachita and shut themselves up in their dark houses.

"Would you turn that obnoxious noise down so I can think?" she said.

"What are you thinking about?" He turned the volume down a notch. "Whose head you're going to put on a platter first?"

"I already know that—the man who serviced my car in Dallas." She swiveled to look behind her. "Did you try that garage back there?"

"I whistled twice, but it didn't come."

"Cute."

"I'm as eager to end this liaison as you are. The garage is closed, but I did spot a motel around the corner."

"Is it clean?"

"If it's not, I'm sure they'll give you a mop and a bucket."

With Bea sitting in stoic silence beside him, Russ turned down a narrow side street and drove toward the flashing neon lights. He stopped in front of a dingy motel office.

Bea sat very still, trying not to feel defeated. Orange and green lights played across her face, proclaiming that there was a vacancy in Paradise. She used an old trick from her childhood, one that always made her feel better: she pretended she was in a meadow filled with sunshine and flowers.

"I suppose this is the end of the line." She even managed a smile.

" 'Parting is such sweet sorrow.' "

Russ surprised himself by liking her smile. He didn't want to like her smile, so he hurried out of the truck and began to unhook her car. She got out on the other side and unloaded her suitcase. She waited on the cracked, dusty sidewalk.

"Well, Toots—" Russ joined her "—it looks like there's somebody in the office to get you settled for the night."

Bea pulled her billfold out of her purse. "How much do I owe you?"

"Let's see. I reckon I used about five dollars worth of gas."

"You come cheap." She handed him a twenty.

"Since you entertained me so royally, and since I don't have any change, we'll call it even." He tucked the money back into her hand.

"We made a deal."

"I changed my mind. Chivalry might be ailing, but it's not dead yet." He climbed into his truck and waved out the window. "See you, Toots."

He left her standing there in her high-heeled pumps and black garbardine skirt with her suitcase at her feet, left her with the neon playing over her cool white blouse and her cool white skin. He thought he could leave her and never look back, but it didn't turn out that way. He glanced in his rearview mirror just as she was lifting her head and squaring her shoulders. Guilt smote him. What if there were no vacancies at that motel? The sign could be wrong. And what about tomorrow? What if her car needed parts? The little garage he'd seen wouldn't have parts for a foreign car. Why did he care?

His brakes squealed as he stopped the truck and made a U-turn in the middle of the road. His fingers tapping the rhythm to Hank Williams's "Jambalaya," he headed back to Paradise.

"Well, now, if it don't look like bizness is pickin' up." The man behind the motel's reception desk smiled at Russ, his square, freckled face pleating with wrinkles. He blew dust off the counter and picked up a pen. "What can I do for you, sir?"

"The lady who just checked in? Bea Adams?"

"Yep. 'Bout five minutes ago."

"I'd like an adjoining room."

The freckled-faced man laughed. "This is your lucky day, feller. Ain't but one room left, and that's Number Three. Right next to Number Two."

"She's in Number Two?"

"I ain't supposed to tell, but seein' as how you left her here and seein' as how you know her name and all, I guess it won't do no harm."

"I guarantee it."

Russ took his modest belongings and settled into room Number Three. He tossed his duffle bag onto a chair and his ice chest onto the floor; then he settled back on the rickety bed with his hands behind his head, looking up at the ceiling, counting the water spots and thinking. He didn't want her to know he'd come back to watch after her. When he saw her in the morning, he'd just say he got tired and decided to spend the night himself. That would do. It sounded casual and uninvolved.

And, heaven knew, involvement was the last thing in the world he wanted. He'd learned that lesson the hard way. And not just from Lurlene. As a matter of fact, Lurlene was a mistake he never should have made. He knew better, had known better since he was eight years old. All those years, going from one foster home to the next, getting his hopes up each time, thinking, "This time I've found a real home."

But it always turned out the same. Just when he would get to loving a new set of parents, he'd be moved to another home.

Finally, his third foster father told him why. He was not worth all the trouble it took to keep him. And besides that, he was too small to earn his keep in the cotton field. He had been eight years old when he'd learned that lesson. He'd also found out that he wasn't in all those homes because of love: he was there because of money. His foster parents were being *paid* to feed, clothe and shelter him.

When he'd been taken out of that home and placed in another, he'd asked the welfare worker if she wouldn't pay his next family enough money so they'd *love* him, too.

She didn't have an answer. He supposed there were no answers. It was best not to even think about it, best to keep on moving, best not to stop long enough to make a connection.

One night wouldn't hurt. One night didn't add up to involvement.

Russ turned his attention to his surroundings. The room was small and musty smelling, decorated with 1950s plastic-laminated furniture and Spanish paintings on velvet. He'd been in worse. And it was cheap. He'd be willing to bet the TV was black-and-white.

Whistling "Your Cheatin' Heart," he got up from the bed and pulled a dog-eared book out of his duffle bag. He'd read until he got sleepy.

He pushed his duffle bag off the chair and settled in, propping his feet on the footboard of the bed. Sounds of running water came from the next room. Bea was taking a shower. He wouldn't even think about that— her naked with water beading her skin. Thinking of women with soft, wet skin was too much temptation. And temptation led to connections.

The water stopped. There was a short silent interval, then the sound of the TV. He couldn't hear the words, just the noise, muted as if it were coming from under a blanket.

He read for a while. Five minutes or fifteen, he didn't know how long. Then he became aware of another sound. He cocked his head, listening. The sound was soft and muffled. At first he thought it was coming from her TV. He got out of his chair and pressed his ear against the thin wall. Bea Adams was crying.

"Well, I'll be damned." He left his post at the wall and paced the floor. He'd never have pegged her as the crying type. Women's tears melted his heart. What in the world was he going to do?

On his second circuit of the small room, his foot banged against the ice chest. Food. There was no telling how long it had been since she'd eaten. He was getting hungry himself.

He opened his ice chest and surveyed his stock—two packs of crackers, one good-sized hunk of cheese, a jar of peanut butter, one loaf of aging bread, three chocolate cookies, four apples and a bottle of cheap wine. It would do.

He made his selection, planned his approach, then left his room.

Bea was on a crying jag.

She sat in the middle of her sagging bed, her head wrapped in a towel, her robe loosely knotted around her waist and her face streaked with tears. The star-crossed lovers danced across the TV screen, sharing one last moment of pleasure before the hero's outraged father came to tear them apart. Bea cried for ill-fated love; she cried for the handsome desert prince; she cried for his beautiful slave-girl lover; and she cried for her toe. She'd cut it on the edge of a broken tile in the bathroom, and it was hurting. She hated pain.

When she heard the knock, she thought it came from the ancient TV. It sounded again, and she realized someone was knocking on her door. She decided to ignore it. She didn't know a soul in Pearcy, Arkansas.

The knock came again, louder this time. Maybe it was the motel manager, coming to tell her to check her mattress for mice before she went to bed. Knotting her belt tighter, she went to the door.

"Who is it?"

"It's me. Russ Hammond. Open up and let me in."

A feeling of relief swept over her. She hadn't realized how forlorn and abandoned she'd felt until she heard the sound of a familiar voice. It didn't matter that the voice belonged to a man she couldn't abide. What mattered was that she was no longer alone and in pain in a strange, remote town. Granted, the pain was small, but that didn't count.

She wiped the tears from her face and opened the door. Russ was leaning against the door frame, holding a bottle of wine in one hand and a hunk of cheese in the other. One snakeskin boot was propped on a small ice chest.

"I can see this is instant attraction between us, sweetheart," he drawled. "But you'll just have to fight it off."

"What took you so long, Big Tex? I was beginning to think I'd have to plow the back forty all by myself."

Russ laughed. He'd never have guessed that she had a playful side.

"I thought you might be hungry," he said.

"I'm famished."

She took the wine and cheese, then held the door open with a bare foot while he brought in the ice chest. He set the chest on a small table under the window, fiddling with it longer than necessary, giving himself time to get used to being in a woman's bedroom again.

"You came back," she said.

She was standing near the bed with the overhead light shining down on her hair. She had taken the towel off, and her dark hair was still damp, as shiny and black as a bird's wing. Traces of tears were on her cheeks.

"I decided I was tired of traveling. It was easier to come back to Pearcy than look for another town."

Now that the initial joy of seeing a familiar face was over, Bea brought herself back under control. It wouldn't do to let him know she was glad to see him. He might take it as interest in checking his chassis.

"Do you always take the easy way?" she asked.

"Always."

He was glad to see her stinger again. She looked so feminine and vulnerable in her white terry robe and her tear-streaked face that she was beginning to make cracks in the wall he'd built around himself. He turned to the ice chest and lifted out a pack of crackers.

Holding them aloft, he turned back to her.

"You have the cheese and I have the crackers. Why don't we get together?"

"I'd consort with a rattlesnake for a bite of food."

"Python, sweetheart." He propped his boot on the bed. "Python."

He quickly surveyed her room. It was exactly like his, except for the velvet pictures. Hers were Italian instead of Spanish. And her chair was covered with her coat instead of a duffle bag. He guessed she'd stashed her suitcase neatly in the small closet. She'd be the type.

He sat on her bed, propped himself up against the headboard and patted a space beside him.

"Join me and we'll break bread together."

Bea hesitated only a moment. It wouldn't be wise to make a fuss. After all, *he* had the food.

"Let me get a dry towel to catch the cracker crumbs."

She disappeared into the bathroom and came back with two plastic cups and a white towel, standard motel issue, dingy from too many careless washings. She spread the towel in the middle of the bed, then sat carefully on her side.

"You look uncomfortable," he said. "Why don't you lean back?"

"This is fine."

"You can't see the TV turned that way."

"I can if I turn my head a little." She demonstrated, glancing over her shoulder at the swashbuckling romance still in progress.

"I don't have plans to ravish you, if that's what you're worried about."

"Ravishment takes two, and I'm not the submissive type." She flounced around and leaned her back against the headboard. She *could* see the TV better. And she didn't want to miss the end of the movie.

"What were you watching?" Russ poured the wine.

"An old movie. They're a weakness of mine."

"Why do you call them a weakness?"

"Most of them are silly. A waste of time." She glanced toward the TV, then back at Russ. "In this one, Tony Curtis is a prince. Nobody can play them the way he can."

"I like that costume the woman is wearing."

"You would." It was a harem suit, showing lots of flesh.

She sipped her wine and concentrated on the movie. It was getting to another good part: the prince was rounding up his consorts to rescue the slave girl from the clutches of his evil father. Catching her lower lip between her teeth, Bea leaned forward.

"Go for it," she whispered.

Russ watched her. He hadn't planned to, but he couldn't help himself. She was flushed with excitement, her skin shining like a pearl. She looked vulnerable, cuddly even. No, he corrected himself. Not cuddly. Bea Adams was far too bossy and waspish to be cuddly.

He turned his attention to the screen. The prince stormed the camp, sword flashing. There was a brief, bloody battle, and then the lovers were reunited. He heard a sniffle.

Out of the corner of his eyes, he caught Bea wiping a tear from her cheek.

"Do you always cry at romantic movies?"

"I wasn't crying." Bea sniffed again and squared her shoulders. "It's the wine, I guess. Allergies. Or maybe fatigue." She made a big to-do of yawning.

Russ didn't know why he wanted to hear the truth from her, but he did. So he pushed.

"It looked like crying to me."

"All right. You caught me." She sat up straighter, as if she wanted to dispel any notion that she might be weak. "Sometimes I cry at romantic movies. And don't ask me why. I certainly don't believe in love."

She looked so spunky and brave, as if she would march out of her dingy hotel room and into battle at any minute, armed with nothing more than tearstains on her cheeks. Tenderness rose up in him, but he dared not let it show. He couldn't afford to get softhearted over a woman's tears.

"Don't worry. No one will ever accuse you of such a heinous crime."

His words stung. She chewed her cheese in silence while she tried to think of a suitable retort.

"I didn't say it was a crime," she said finally. "I merely said I don't believe in love. Do you?"

"No." Her question caught him off guard. "I did once, but not anymore."

"What happened? Did somebody get tired of your snakeskin boots and throw you out the door with them?"

Everything in Russ shut down. His eyes became shuttered, his face lost its animation, even his body went stiff and cold, as if a giant hand had snuffed out the fires that kept him warm.

He got off the bed. The bedsprings squeaked in protest.

"Do you want any more food? Wine?" He sounded like a disinterested waiter.

"No, thank you."

"Then I'll take them and go on back to my room."

Bea regretted her last remark, but she didn't know how to take it back without making matters worse. "It was kind of you to bring them over." She got off the bed. "I'll pay for my half."

"It's Sunday. On Sundays I'm generous."

He quickly repacked his ice chest. Watching him, Bea suddenly felt cold. She pulled her robe closer around her neck. "Russ." He turned around. "I don't think I ever thanked you properly for helping me."

"I wouldn't want you to miss an opportunity to do things the proper way."

She sucked in a quick, angry breath. "Why don't you take your ice chest and your python boots and leave before one of us dies from assault with a deadly tongue?"

"Good idea. Don't bother to show me the door. I know the way out." Whistling "Your Cheatin' Heart," he headed for the door. "Good night now, Toots."

As soon as the door closed behind him, she kicked the bed. She had forgotten that her feet were bare and that she'd already hurt her toe. Tears of pain and frustration stung her eyes, and she hobbled to the bathroom, muttering to herself.

"Any woman can make a fool of herself over a man, but only I could make a fool of myself over a drifter. It must be in my genes."

She stuck her foot in the lavatory sink and turned on the cold-water tap. Tepid water came out.

"Can't even get cold water when I need it." Grabbing a cloth, she pressed it against the broken skin. She could still hear him whistling that dreadful song.

Taking her foot out of the sink, she banged on the wall. The whistling stopped. Then came a soft tapping.

"Sending me signals, sweetheart?" His voice was faint through the walls, but she could make out the words. "If you want me, use Morse code. S.O.S." He started whistling again.

"Hell will freeze over before I'll send you a signal." She listened. There was no reply this time, but the whistling had stopped.

With her toe wrapped in the washcloth, she hobbled back to her bed. The movie credits were showing on the black-and-white TV.

"He even made me miss the end of the movie."

She fluffed up her pillow and settled back to see what was playing on the late show. The theme music sounded like horror. She leaned forward as the title came up on the screen: *Creature from the Black Lagoon*.

Good. She needed two hours of slime and screams to take her mind off her own horror show: that aggravating blond pirate next door and his infernal country-and-western music.

Chapter Three

Russ always woke up early.

He didn't need an alarm clock. His inner clock was fine-tuned to the sun. He showered and dressed with the quick efficiency of a man on the move. Then he picked up his book, sat in his chair and waited.

Sounds of movement came from Bea's room sooner than he'd expected. Either she was an early riser or she was anxious to get on with her business. He waited until he heard her leave her room, waited until she had time to get to the motel office; then he loaded his gear into his truck and followed her. *Just to make sure,* he told himself, although he didn't know exactly what he was making sure of.

She was standing at the dusty counter, dressed in high heels and a smart green wool suit, looking for all the world like the high-powered Dallas advertising executive she was. He didn't know why he'd ever thought she might need him around to take care of her.

He couldn't change what was done, though. He might as well go inside and check out.

"We have to stop meeting this way, Toots."

She turned around slowly and acknowledged him with a brief nod. Everything about her was cool and elegant: the way she moved, the way she looked, the way she talked.

"Checking out, Mr. Hammond?"

"After you," he said.

"How a good night's sleep does improve your manners."

"Some of us got lucky."

He meandered across the room and sat on a green plastic sofa to wait his turn. The early-morning sun set dust motes to dancing. He knocked a cobweb off a copy of *Progressive Farmer* magazine and turned to a scintillating article on boll weevils. Although he didn't plan to get involved in the problems of Miss Beatrice Adams this morning, he couldn't help but overhear the conversation between her and the desk clerk, a bony female with an Ichabod Crane nose and a Betty Davis hairdo. Ivalene Crump, her plastic name tag had said.

"Miss Crump, can you please tell me if there is a place that serves breakfast?"

"There's just one. Freddy's General Store."

"The general store?"

"Yep. 'Course Freddy has nails and hunk cheese and fabric by the bolt, but a couple a' years back he set up a little hot plate and a little oven behind the ceramic whatnots and started cooking up biscuits and ham. Raises and kills his own hogs. Makes the best redeye gravy in Arkansas."

Russ looked over the top of his magazine at Bea. He'd have to give her credit. She didn't blink an eye at the story of the enterprising Freddy.

"I see." Bea squared her shoulders. It was the same gesture he'd seen her use last night. He supposed she did it when she needed to plump up her courage. It would have been heartwarming, if he had a heart. "Well...tell me another thing," she was saying. "Do you have cab service in Pearcy?"

"Cabs?"

"Taxi cabs...a bus, any type of public transportation?"

"Lordy, this is not Little Rock. But we manage anyhow. The bus runs, but not very regular. Sometimes Purdy Dillard lets folks hitch a ride on his mail truck— that is, if you can catch him, and you already missed him."

"Then perhaps I can use your phone to call the garage."

Russ dropped the magazine back in the rack and stood up. "I'm going in that direction. I'll be glad to give you one last tow."

"I wouldn't dream of putting you to that trouble."

"I'm going that way anyhow. I have to get gas before I move on."

Bea was proud, but she was not foolish. She'd do what was necessary to get home the quickest way possible.

"It seems I'm obliged to accept your help one more time, Russ Hammond."

"Fate must have a sense of humor."

"Or a mean streak."

Russ laughed as he joined her at the counter to check out. Afterward, he made quick work of hooking up her car for another tow.

"I'm getting good at this," he remarked. "I guess I could make it my life's work."

"What *is* your work?"

"I do odd jobs when the mood strikes me or when the cash runs low, whichever comes first."

"You're not vacationing?"

"Hardly." He finished fastening their vehicles together, then opened the passenger door of his truck. "Your chariot awaits."

Bea climbed in. The truck looked worse in the daylight than it did in the dark. Rust spots showed in patches on the fenders, and the seats had places where the vinyl had peeled. She made up her mind that she would pay him this time, no matter what he said. *Odd jobs, how strange.* In spite of appearances, she had decided he was merely eccentric, a professor suffering burnout or perhaps a businessman who got his kicks bumming around. Of course, she had come to that conclusion in the middle of the horror movie, so her mind hadn't exactly been in its most elevated state. Still, he sounded educated. *Don't be a snob, Bea,* she chided herself, *some lazy people do go to school.*

"Where to first?" The slamming door rocked the old truck as Russ climbed in on the driver's side. "Breakfast or the garage?"

"I'd like to get my car repaired as quickly as possible."

"The garage, then."

He was silent as he drove. She wished he'd whistle: it made him easier to dismiss. For all his faults, she was beginning to see a good side to Russ Hammond. There was an innate kindness about him. Whether he knew it or not, he was going out of his way to be her guardian angel. He'd tried to be casual, to make everything look like coincidence—coming back to the motel, showing up with the cheese and wine, checking out when she did—but she was too smart to believe in so much coincidence.

She didn't want to see a good side to Russ Hammond. Looking out the window at the sights of Pearcy, she sighed.

"What's the matter?" He glanced her way. "Do you have the blues?"

"I never have the blues."

"I guess you'd consider them a weakness—like crying at romantic movies."

"I never have any philosophical discussions on an empty stomach."

"As soon as we drop off your car, we'll eat."

"I thought you had to be moving on."

"A man has to eat sometime. It might as well be in Pearcy."

"I'm glad you said that. For a moment, I thought you were beginning to enjoy my company."

"A little vinegar is invigorating every now and then, but I prefer sugar, myself."

She'd never been called vinegar. But then, she'd never met a man like Russ.

They arrived at the garage just as the doors were being unlocked. While Russ pumped gas, Bea arranged to leave her car for repair. She even managed to convince the slow-talking, slow-moving mechanic, Hal Lindley, that she needed it in a hurry. Russ returned from the gas pump in time to hear her telling the mechanic she *had* to get to Florence, Alabama, for a family reunion. The mechanic nodded in sympathy. Apparently, family reunions were something he understood.

"I'll take a look see while you eat breakfast," he finally said.

Breakfast turned out to be surprisingly good, even if they did have to sit on two up-ended crates and balance their food on a wooden cracker barrel. On a whim, Bea bought Russ a rubber doll in a hula skirt to hang on his rearview mirror.

"To keep you entertained after I'm gone," she said, handing it to him as they climbed back into his truck.

He laughed at the way the doll shimmied when he took it by the string. Bea kept surprising him.

He suspended his dancing rubber doll, then headed back to the garage. The mechanic emerged from underneath the Jaguar with bad news.

"I don't carry parts for these foreign-built cars," he told Bea. "Too expensive. And besides that, I don't get too many of them here in Pearcy." He showed two chipped teeth when he laughed.

"Is there anyone nearby who is equipped to work on my car?"

"I can do the work. I just don't have the parts." Hal pushed his greasy cap back and scratched the top of his head. "Let's see now . . . the closest dealership is Memphis."

Bea's journey home was taking on all the complications of an expedition to the North Pole. She conjured up her sunlit meadow once more as she discussed the many possibilities of repairing her car with Pearcy's only mechanic. She finally decided the most sensible thing to do was leave it in Pearcy and let him order the parts from Memphis. She could pick it up on the way back to Dallas.

That left the problem of getting home in time for her family's reunion. Mainly, she just wanted to go home for a soothing, healing visit with her mother and her brother, but the reunion was important, too. Bea had discovered that the older she got, the more important roots were to her. Besides that, she was too stubborn to admit defeat. She'd be darned if she'd let a broken car stop her from attending her family reunion.

Russ was leaning against a stack of old tires, whistling some infernal country song while she asked about rental cars.

"Lord-ee, lady." The mechanic laughed and slapped his thigh. "Who'd want to rent a car in Pearcy?"

"I do."

"Well, this ain't Little Rock."

"So I've been told." She squared her shoulders and tried again. "What's the nearest town that might have a car-rental agency?"

Russ listened to the towns the mechanic named: Hot Springs, Little Rock, Jacksonville. He didn't know why he was still hanging around. His job was done. He'd seen her and her car safely to the garage. He'd even seen that she had a proper breakfast, if you could call red-eye gravy proper. And he did. He didn't know what time it was, but it felt late. Ordinarily he'd have been on the road by this time of morning, heading toward a strange town, any town without orange groves and a sky so blue it hurt your eyes to look at it—any town that wasn't LaBelle, Florida.

He shifted his weight away from the tires and started toward the door. He didn't even owe Bea a goodbye.

He'd honk his horn and wave when he got into his truck.

As he reached the door, he heard Bea inquiring if anyone in Pearcy could be hired to drive her into Hot Springs. Russ kept on walking. It wasn't his problem anymore. Bea was a resourceful woman. She'd handle whatever needed to be handled.

He already had the key in the ignition when he made a fatal mistake. He took one last look through the garage door. Something about the determined set of Bea's shoulders made him think of a little girl playing grown-up. He knew what he was going to do. He didn't stop to question his motives. He didn't want to even *think* about his motives.

With one hand still on the wheel, he leaned over and rambled through the truck pocket till he found his map. He consulted it quickly and stuffed it back in the pocket. Then he pulled the key from the ignition, opened the door, got out of his truck and went back into the garage.

"I'll take you home."

"What?" Bea turned around to face him.

"I said, I'll take you home."

"I heard what you said." Her voice softened. "I just don't know why you said it."

"You need to get home and I need an odd job."

"It would be odd, all right. The two of us traveling together in your pickup truck."

"The Odd Couple?"

"Worse. *Who's Afraid of Virginia Woolf?"*

"I don't recall a Virginia Woolf in these parts," Hal interrupted, scratching his head and looking at the two of them as if they had lost their minds. "Is she any kin to the Woolfs up around Heber Springs?"

"I don't think so." Bea held back her smile. "Did you think of anyone who could drive me into Hot Springs?"

"Like I was saying, I might could take you over that way myself, but it'd be sometime this afternoon 'fore I could get loose here."

Bea considered her options. If she waited for Hal, she'd lose almost an entire day. And she'd already lost one. Uncle Mack and Aunt Rachel would arrive in Florence tomorrow. The rest of her relatives would be there the day after—Wednesday. That's when the reunion started. She didn't want to miss a thing. Going home was more than a visit with her family. It was more than a reunion with distant kin. Going home was an odyssey of renewal. Bea's roots were deep in the red clay of northwest Alabama. She took her strength from the soil and from the stalwart people she called kin.

"I accept your offer, Russ Hammond. You can drive me home, and I'll refill your sagging coffers. It will be business straight down the line. Deal?" She held out her hand. He took it.

"Deal." Her hand had a soft, boneless feel that was unexpectedly feminine, though why it was unexpected, he couldn't say. He held it longer than he meant to and longer than he should have. The slight flush that came into her cheeks told him so. He released her hand. "Well, let's get this show on the road."

He transferred her suitcase to the back of his pickup while she made arrangements to return for her car on Saturday. Then he escorted her to his truck and opened the door for her. Her slim skirt jacked over her knees as she climbed into the cab. Her legs were feminine, too, he noticed. Slim and nicely curved.

He was irritated at himself for noticing and tried to cover with conversation. "That's not much of an outfit for traveling," he said. "Don't you want to change into something more comfortable?"

"This *is* comfortable." Bea settled onto the seat. "There's no sense in taking on sloppy habits just because I'm traveling."

"I guess one man's sloppiness is another man's comfort. I call these comfortable."

Russ ran a hand absently down the thigh of his faded blue jeans. Bea tried not to notice, but she couldn't help herself. He had such a fine body. If he'd been deliberately flaunting it, she could have handled him with disdain. But the sensuous movement had been entirely unconscious. She was sure of that.

She caught her lower lip between her teeth and turned to stare out the windshield.

"Don't you think we should be leaving? It's going to be a long drive, and I'd like to get home tonight if we can."

Russ came around and climbed behind the wheel. "You can forget tonight. This old baby won't make the time your Jag did, and there's no sense driving into the night. If everything goes well, I'd say you'll be home sometime tomorrow morning."

"What about tonight?"

The loud rattling of the truck almost drowned out her question. Russ idled the engine, letting it warm up before he answered.

"I usually camp out when I'm on the road."

"I hate camping."

"That's fine with me. I have only one sleeping bag anyhow."

He revved the engine and reached for the radio at the same time. Twangy country music filled the truck. Bea's stomach lurched, and for a minute she thought she was going to lose her breakfast. Already she was regretting her decision to let this drifter take her home. But she was determined to make the best of it.

"Since I'm footing the bill, I suggest we stop for the night in a motel."

"Whatever you say." He pursed his lips to whistle along with the music, then changed his mind and winked at her. "We'll find another Paradise."

"I sincerely hope not."

They left the garage with a loud fanfare. The truck backfired and rattled with a vengeance. Bea held her peace.

Soon the little town of Pearcy was behind them. They rode in silence. Without saying so, both of them understood that silence was the best way for them to get along.

Bea's toe began to twinge, and she thought about slipping her shoe off to give the pain some room; but she quickly rejected that notion. Pulling off her shoes would be a comfortable, even intimate gesture. She didn't want Russ getting the idea that she was comfortable around him, and she certainly didn't want him to entertain the idea that she harbored feelings of intimacy. She kept her shoes on and suffered.

Glancing down at her watch, she saw that it was already eleven o'clock.

"It seems to me we should be off these winding mountain back roads by now," she said.

"I prefer traveling the back roads. It's more scenic."

"I'm not interested in the scenery. I want to get home."

"Maybe you should try clicking your ruby-red slippers, Dorothy."

"Don't you ever take anything seriously?"

He glanced her way. If he hadn't, she would never have seen his eyes. For an instant she saw pain peering from the depths of all that deep blue innocence. The look vanished quickly, though, and he was once more the careless maverick.

"Not anymore." He turned his face back to the road. "However, since you're footing the bill, I don't want you worried that you aren't getting your money's worth. I'll meander toward a super highway with generic scenery as soon as we get down out of these mountains."

There was a loud grinding sound and then ominous silence. The engine stopped, the radio went dead, and even the whistling quit.

"Just like a dead fish in the water," Russ said, settling back in his seat.

"I would have said a dead whale, but to each his own."

Bea checked her watch again. Five after eleven. Russ was sitting on his side of the truck with his head leaned back and his eyes closed.

"You're napping? At a time like this?"

He opened one eye and glanced her way. "This happens occasionally. The truck shuts down and takes a little rest." He folded his arms across his chest and shut his eyes again. "I suggest you do the same."

"I'm not a truck." He chuckled. "I fail to see the humor in this situation." She tapped her fingers against the dashboard. "Aren't you going to even see what's the matter?"

"Vapor lock, so I've been told. There's nothing to do but wait for the truck to cool off."

"At this rate, I'll probably get to Florence in time to help truss the Thanksgiving turkey."

"You don't relax much, do you?" Russ didn't even look her way. If he hadn't been talking, she might have thought he was asleep. Or dead. He was that still.

Bea didn't even bother to reply. If anything was going to be done to remedy the situation, she'd have to do it herself. She got out and hobbled around the truck, looking for signs of a breakdown. Her toe was hurting in earnest now. The way her luck was running, she figured her mind would go next.

A suspicious puff of smoke wafted from under the hood. *Aha. A visible sign of trouble.* If she could get under there and take a look, she might be able to fix it. It was an old truck. She thought she could lift the hood by releasing some kind of latch underneath it. She rounded the front of the truck and reached toward the hood.

"Don't." Strong hands gripped her shoulders and pulled her back.

She twisted her head and looked over her shoulder at Russ's face. He was furious.

"What in the hell kind of fool trick are you trying to pull? Don't you know you can get burned?" He still had her in a tight grip.

"Let go of me." She didn't even consider struggling. She was accustomed to having her orders obeyed. "I'm not some spoiled, silly child."

"Then stop acting like one."

He turned her around so that they were face to face. His hands bit into the tender flesh at the top of her arms and a tight muscle jumped in the side of his jaw.

Why in the world was he so angry? If he expected her to feel chastised or foolish, he was completely mistaken. She lifted her chin and stared straight into his eyes. Something moved there. A flame of recognition.

Bea sucked in her breath. Suddenly she was aware of the way his body touched hers, of the feel of hard thighs against her wool skirt and solid muscle against her suit jacket. The rhythm of her heart increased and she felt a little light-headed. It was pure animal attraction.

Like father, like daughter. Bea was disgusted with herself. Unconsciously, she flicked her tongue over her lips.

"I thought you were asleep." She tried to make her voice commanding, but she was failing miserably. There was no sane reason why she should sound like one of those sappy heroines on a late-night movie. "I didn't see you get out. Why aren't you still in the truck?"

He didn't answer her immediately. He couldn't. He was vividly, achingly aware of her as a woman. She felt soft under his hands, and pliant. He hadn't had a woman since Lurlene. How long had that been? Two years? Two and a half? All that deprivation was making him soft in the head.

He eased his grip. He hadn't realized he'd been holding her so tightly.

"Did I hurt you?"

"No."

He released her and stepped back. She crossed her arms and hugged herself, putting her hands on the exact spot he had touched.

"Are you cold?"

"Just a little chilly. I had thought it was hotter today." She rubbed her arms.

"There's nothing you can do out here, Bea. The truck will take twenty or thirty minutes to cool off, and then we'll be on our way again."

It was the first time he'd ever called her anything except Toots or Tiger Lady or Boopsy or Sweetheart. For some reason, his use of her name made her feel friendlier toward him. And that scared her a little.

"Why didn't you tell me so in the first place?"

"I guess it's because I like to see your stinger."

"I thought you didn't like vinegar."

"Sometimes its refreshing."

Bea shivered, and not entirely from the cold. Russ took her elbow and guided her back toward the truck.

"Let's wait inside where it's warmer," he said.

She allowed herself to be led, but somehow she didn't feel foolish or childish or even dominated. She merely felt protected. It was a strange feeling. She wasn't sure whether she liked it or not. And since she didn't know, she walked beside him without further protest, favoring her sore toe as she moved.

"You're limping." He stopped and looked down at her as if she had committed a major crime.

"It's just a sore toe. I cut it last night on the bathroom tile."

"Did you clean the wound? Did you use an antibiotic salve?"

"Good grief. What are you? A doctor?"

A man who has lost too much. The thought floated across his mind like a ghost. He saw all the people in his life, drifting away from him one by one, dissolving in a mist at the precise moment he reached out to them. His mother and daddy, sitting in a swing under a grape arbor, laughing at the frog house he'd built in the sandpile nearby, laughing, laughing and suddenly vanishing

from his life when he was five years old. Killed, he'd
found out later, in a senseless car accident. And the
foster families—Sarah and Clem Robbins, Martha and
James Lotharp, Robbie Sue and Michael Lansky. The
list went on and on. Even the dog he'd had once, Old
Rex, dead and bloated from snake bite after only two
weeks of playing catch in the pasture at twilight. And
finally, Lurlene.

"Russ?" Bea said. He didn't seem to hear her. She
put her hand on his cheek. "Russ? Are you all right?"

Unconsciously he covered her hand, pressing it close
against his skin. He needed to be touched. With sudden clarity he knew that the human touch was healing.
Why, suddenly, was this sharp-witted, independent
woman the one to make him see that need?

He mentally shook himself. Because he was still
holding her hand against his face, and because he didn't
want her to get the wrong idea—or any ideas at all—he
put on a performance. Bending at the waist like a Brit-
ish fop, he planted an exaggerated kiss in her palm.
Then he gave her a broad wink.

"Tiger Lady, the thought of harm coming to even
one hair on your head fills me with woe. Let one drop
of blood ooze from your lily-white skin, and I tremble
with fear."

"I deserve every bit of your undying devotion."

He straightened up and grinned at her.

"You do?"

"Certainly I do. I'm paying for it."

He could have told her that money didn't buy devotion. Instead, he laughed. The mountains caught the
sound and bounced it back to them. Bea joined him.

"What did I tell you?" he said. *"Who's Afraid of
Virginia Woolf."*

"I'm the one who said that."

"At least you got something right." Without thinking about his actions or their consequences, he scooped her into his arms and carried her to the truck. She allowed that, too.

"Tell me if this is going to be a ravishment. I need to powder my nose."

"It's not your nose I'm worried about. It's your foot." He plumped her inside the truck and sat down beside her.

"You're worried?"

"If anything happens to you, I won't get paid."

"You're mercenary right down to the cockles of your cold heart."

"Guilty. Now take off your shoe."

"I thought ravishments usually started with the blouse."

She gave him a look that would have melted a suit of armor. It was a deliciously sexy look that was totally uncontrived. He was certain of that. He was equally certain she was unaware of what she had done.

Suddenly all the repartee between them took on new dimensions. *Ravishment.* She had used the word. He was amazed to realize that on that deserted mountain road in the tight confines of his pickup truck, the idea of ravishing her didn't sound so absurd. To feel her yielding body under his. To run his hands over her cool white skin. To press his lips against the fluttering pulse point of her throat.

He must be going mad.

Without a word, he reached for her leg. Surprisingly, she made no protest. His hand circled her calf. Her silk stockings whispered as he slid his hand down toward her shoe. He caught the back of her pump and slipped it from her foot. The shoe clunked softly onto the floorboard and lay on its side, unnoticed.

Russ lifted her foot and put it in his lap. It was slim and small, much smaller than he would have expected for such a tall woman.

"Russ?" Bea caught her lower lip between her teeth as he swiveled his head to look at her. His eyes held hers for a long, slow heartbeat, then he turned his attention back to her foot.

"I had to see for myself." He gently probed her toe through the silk stocking. She didn't wince; she didn't move. "I wouldn't want anything to happen to you, Tiger Lady. Life's more interesting when you're around."

Chapter Four

Bea expelled a long breath. For a moment, when his hand had been warm on her leg through her silk stockings, she had thought he was trying to seduce her. And she had been more than half-willing. The idea shocked her.

She had always been in complete charge of her relationships with men, even to the manner of their departure, if her friend Margaret was to be believed. They were always mannerly and polite around her. And they never, never crossed the lines that she drew.

Russ did. Not only did he cross the lines, he pretended he didn't even see them. He insulted her, aggravated her and *touched* her in ways that she had never allowed. And yet... right now, with her foot resting in his lap, she couldn't dismiss him as a lazy rambling man. He was more, so much more. He was witty, intelligent, complex and extraordinarily appealing.

The appealing part was almost her undoing.

"It's just a small cut." Her voice wasn't as strong as she wanted it to be. She tried again. "I don't think it's fatal."

"Nevertheless..." He ceased talking in order to bend over her toe. His breath was warm against her leg. She shivered. "The skin is broken." He ran his finger gently over the cut. "There is some swelling." He lifted accusing eyes to hers. "What do you think you are? Invincible?"

"It's only a toe."

"A toe is part of the body. Don't you know infection can spread?"

His hands were hot. She could feel their heat on her leg.

"I'll take care of it tomorrow, when I get home."

"No. I'll do it now. Pull off your stockings."

"What?"

"Are you going to do it, or shall I do it for you?"

He had gone too far. Feeling friendly toward him was one thing; being ordered around by him was another. She tried to pull her leg away. He held it fast.

"If you think this is a ploy to see your legs, you're wrong." His face was fierce and his eyes were intensely blue as he leaned closer to her. "I'm not interested in your legs or any other part of your beautiful body. We made a business deal, and this is business. I plan to deliver you to Florence in one piece." He released her leg and stepped out of the truck. Before he shut the door, he gave her one last order. "Now, pull off those stockings so I can take care of your toe."

He slammed the door shut for emphasis and walked away. He was proud of his control. Except for that slip about her body being beautiful, he'd maintained the aloofness he'd wanted. Of course, he shouldn't have carried her, either, but that didn't count. Nothing counted until they had gotten into the truck. Then things had heated up between them. *Deprivation.* That's all it could be. He hadn't had a woman since Lurlene. Hadn't wanted a woman. Hadn't needed a woman. Until today.

He rammed his hands into his pockets and stared into the timeless Quachita Mountains. No answers there. Just beauty and quietness and a strange kind of peace. He stood on the side of the road and watched the mountains.

Inside the truck, Bea watched him. His passions were tightly controlled. She could tell by the rigid lines of his body. She put her hands on her hot face. Her own passions weren't as well under control. Anger and frustration made her stomach tight and her hands shake. Besides that, she was hot, hot all over. But not from anger and frustration. She was hot for another reason.

Face it, Bea Adams, that bearded pirate has made you hot with desire. She groaned. She had to pull herself together. She had always prided herself on her good judgment. Falling under Russ Hammond's spell would not be good judgment.

"Okay." The sound of her own voice reassured her. "All right." She stiffened her spine and tilted her chin. "I'll pull off my hose and put a bandage on my toe and get the heck off this mountain." In the tight space she wiggled out of her pantyhose. "It's this darned mountain." She shook her hose out, folded them neatly and put them in her purse. She didn't want Russ to see any of her intimate apparel. "And this crazy weather." Clouds had begun to form, making the noonday sky dark.

Bea straightened her skirt and leaned out the window. "I'm ready," she called. Russ turned around. Something in his expression made her regret her choice of words. He looked predatory. "My toe is ready," she amended.

He came back to the truck and rummaged in his duffle bag. Then he climbed in beside her.

"Let me see." He reached for her leg again.

"I can do it." She reached for the tube of salve.

Their hands collided. Both drew back from the touch. She took a deep, shaky breath, and he made a low sound in his throat. Rage, passion, pain. She didn't know how to describe the sound.

"Here." Abruptly he thrust the antibiotic toward her. "Apply the salve generously, then cover it with this." He handed her a box of Band-Aids.

She made quick work of the chore. He wanted not to notice, but he couldn't help himself. He had always loved a woman's bare feet. Bea had a tiny blue vein in the arch of her foot that made her look fragile and vulnerable. He focused on that small patch of blue.

She turned and caught him looking. He didn't flinch, didn't move. Bea felt heat prickles crawl up her leg. For a moment she was mesmerized, and then slowly, ever so slowly she tucked her bare foot under her.

Deprived of the view, Russ lifted his gaze to hers.

"All set?" His voice betrayed nothing.

"Yes." Her voice was shaky.

"Then I think we can get going. The truck should be cool by now." He turned the key, and the truck came to life. With the sky darkening and Bea sitting in silence with her bare feet tucked under her, they continued down the mountain.

The radio had started playing as soon as Russ had turned the key. He turned it off.

"Thank you." Bea gave him a small smile.

"You're welcome."

The first drop of rain spattered against the windshield. Bea watched it with a sort of detachment. She was aware of only two things: the soothing feel of the salve on her toe and the tremendous sexual magnetism of the man sitting beside her. She balled her hands into fists and squeezed so hard her nails bit into her flesh.

"It's raining," she commented, still not really paying much attention to the weather.

"The sky is dark."

"Hmm."

They drove in silence. The rain fell in a fine sprinkle. Then without warning, the sky opened and spilled its contents on the pickup truck. Rain beat so hard against the windshield, Russ could barely see. It battered the roof and lashed the windows.

Bea leaned forward, hugging herself and trying to see through the downpour. *Lord, don't let it thunder,* she said to herself. *Don't let lightning streak the sky.* She was scared to death of thunderstorms. Had been since she was born, she guessed. It was a foolish weakness that she wasn't proud of, and she certainly didn't want to display any more weaknesses before Russ Hammond.

Russ braked the truck, catching Bea's attention.

"My clothes!" Bea said suddenly, looking out the back window. Her suitcase was only a shadow seen darkly through the curtain of rain.

"What?" Russ leaned forward, straining to see.

"My clothes will be soaked. You have to stop."

"They're already wet."

"You don't know that. I have a good, tight suit-case."

"This is a good, hard rain. You don't need to be out in it."

"I want you to stop this truck."

"You are the stubbornest woman I've ever met. You'll get soaked."

"It's my body."

He glanced at her. In the gray light, her face was set in the determined lines he'd come to know so well. He kept going.

"It's also my money."

His jaw tightened. Without another word, he pulled over to the side of the road. She jerked open her door and swung her legs down. He grabbed her around the waist and hauled her back into the truck. Then he leaned over her and slammed the door shut.

"What do you think you're doing?" she asked.

"I don't have any remedies for pneumonia in my duffle bag." He took his handkerchief out of his pants pocket and wiped the water off her legs. A muscle twitched in the side of his jaw. "If you want to get soaked and catch your death of cold, you can wait until you get home to do it."

She sat with her back rigid as he bent over her and dried her legs all the way down to her ankles. She held her breath as he lifted her feet, one by one, and wiped every drop of moisture from them.

The windows were fogged from their breathing. With the dark sky and the steamy windows, she felt as if she were in a cocoon. The feeling wasn't entirely unpleasant.

Russ straightened and tucked the handkerchief back into his pocket.

"Stay here. Don't move."

He pulled his jacket collar up and stepped into the rain. Within seconds he was back. Plopping the wet suitcase onto the seat, he climbed in.

"Thank you."

He didn't reply. Taking his handkerchief out of his pocket, he wiped his face. The damp cloth didn't begin to soak up all the rain he'd collected on his errand of gallantry.

Bea couldn't sit there and watch it any longer.

"Here. Let me do that." She opened her purse and took out a lace-edged linen handkerchief."

She leaned toward him, but the suitcase was in the way. In order to balance, she had to put one hand on his shoulder.

He sat very still as she lifted the tiny material to his face. The sweet scent of flowers wafted under his nose.

"That little piece of material is hardly big enough for a flea." His voice was gruff. It had been a long, long time since anybody had cared enough about him to wipe his face.

"If you have any fleas in this beard, you'd better tell me now. I can't abide fleas."

Her quip lightened the mood. They laughed together.

"Than you'd better let me do that. I haven't looked lately."

He took the handkerchief and finished mopping his face.

She settled back into her seat, glad the suitcase was between them. "Who says there are no good Samaritans anymore? You're a good Samaritan, Russ Hammond."

"Don't tell. My reputation would be ruined." Absently he stuffed her little handkerchief into his pocket. "It looks like the rain is letting up some."

"Can you see well enough to drive?"

"Yes. As long as I watch the speed."

He pulled back onto the mountain road, and they crept along. Their respite lasted twenty minutes, and then the rain began to slash the truck viciously. Russ eased around the mountain curves, peering hard into the rain, trying to spot the potholes in the road in time to avoid a teeth-jarring encounter.

Suddenly Bea caught his arm. "Listen. Do you hear that?"

There was a rumbling sound coming up from the ground, as if the earth were growling its discontent.

"I hear it." Automatically he slowed the truck.

"What is it?"

"It sounds like distant traffic."

The sound became louder. Suddenly Russ knew what it was. Rock slide. It sometimes happened on mountain roads, especially during torrential rains. Judging by the sounds, rocks were tumbling some distance behind them and almost immediately ahead of them. They were trapped.

His jaw tightened and he leaned over the wheel, searching desperately for a place to pull over. Bea saw the change in him, felt the sudden tension.

"Russ?"

He didn't answer her. A muscle twitched in his jaw and his knuckles turned white. He was tired of losing people. Even if Bea was not connected to him in any important way, he'd be damned if he'd let anything happen to her.

"What's wrong, Russ?" Bea gripped his arm.

"Hang on, Bea."

There were no good places to pull off the road. No wide shoulders and safe havens presented themselves. Russ took the only way out. Shifting gears, he plunged off the road and started up a small, rocky incline. The old truck swayed, its tires spinning and squealing, seeking purchase on the slick ground.

Bea's teeth knocked together, and she bounced around on the seat. But she held on. She braced one hand on the dashboard and kept the other one on Russ's upper arm. He felt solid and safe. It was the first time in her life she'd counted on a man to make her feel solid and safe.

The incline leveled off, and Russ swung the truck into the shelter of a copse of trees. He cut the engine and covered her hand.

"Are you all right?"

"Fine." She held on to his arm a while longer, letting the contact, the feeling of togetherness, strengthen her. The distant roar of falling rocks had ceased.

"I think the sound we heard was a rock slide, Bea. Just up ahead. I'll check as soon as the rain slackens."

She shivered. "That makes twice."

"Twice what?"

"Twice you've saved my life. Once from rock slide and once from a fatal cut toe."

The laughter diminished the tension.

"Being trapped in the mountains is not my idea of fun, but I suppose if it had to happen, I'm glad it happened with you, Bea."

"What a nice thing to say."

"It's Monday. I try to be nice on Mondays."

"What about Tuesdays?"

"I live from day to day. I'll let you know when Tuesday comes." He glanced out at the rain, then back at Bea. "I don't suppose you play poker, do you?"

"I happen to be the world's best seven-card stud player."

"We'll see about that."

This time he wasn't even surprised. If Bea Adams had claimed to be a Japanese wrestler, he'd have believed her. He got a deck of cards out of the truck pocket and dealt their hands.

Two hours later, it turned out Bea had been right. She was good enough to beat him at every hand except one.

"It's these damp jeans," he said. "I'm off my game."

"It's your brain. Country music is bound to make a person a little addlepated."

"What do you have against country music?"

She opened her mouth and then closed it without saying a word. *Taylor Adams* had been on the tip of her tongue. She bit back the words. Russ had already wormed his way into her emotions; she'd be darned if she let him work his way into her mind.

"Look." She turned her face to the window. "It has almost stopped raining."

"I'll go check the road."

"I'm coming with you." She reached for the door handle.

"You are not." He reached over and caught her arm.

"I most certainly am." She look pointedly at his hand on her arm. When he didn't take the hint, she gave a direct order. "Take your hands off me. I'm paying you to take me home, not to order me around."

"Those roads are slick out there, and treacherous. What if you fall?"

"I'll get back up."

"You're dressed for a board meeting, not a trek on a wet mountain road."

"I guess I could pull off my suit and go stark naked, but I *am* going."

"Stubborn woman." He released her and got out on his side of the truck, still mad. "How in the hell she ever lived to be a grown woman is a miracle to me. Taking foolhardy chances. She must have a damned guardian angel watching over her." He was still fuming when he came around to her side and opened the door. "Hop down."

He took her elbow to help her out of the truck.

"You can let go. I'm not helpless."

"I can't stop you from going, but I can damned sure stop you from falling off this mountain." He slammed the door harder than he had to. "Now behave yourself."

She didn't protest any more. A hundred yards down the road, she was glad he'd insisted on holding her arm. The roads were muddy and her footing was uncertain. He'd been right. High heels were designed for a boardroom, not mountain climbing.

Around the bend, they discovered the source of the sound they'd heard. A large pile of rocks blocked the road, one or two of them boulder size.

Bea's spirits fell. Another delay. And from the looks of things, this would be a long one.

"Can we move them?" she asked.

"Yes. It will take a while, but I can do it."

"*We* can do it."

"Now how did I know you'd say that?"

"Experience?" She smiled up at him.

It was a smile he couldn't resist. He brushed back her damp hair, letting his hand linger long enough to savor the touch of her soft cheek.

"Experience, Tiger Lady." He was still touching her face, and he was getting ideas again. Quickly he withdrew his hand. "It's way past lunchtime, and I'm hungry. Why don't we eat before we try to do anything?"

They had cheese and apples and two country-ham sandwiches Russ had purchased at Freddy's General Store early that morning. After lunch, Russ set up his tent in the shelter of the trees.

For once Bea didn't insist on helping. She hated camping and knew nothing about tents. She'd only be in the way. She sat on a rock and watched, mindless of the damp. Her wool suit was already ruined, anyway. It was muddy and torn where she had snagged the hem on a prickly bush. Russ had been right about her clothes. She wasn't dressed for traveling in the mountains. She hated for him to be right about so many things. That meant she had been wrong, and she didn't like to be wrong.

As she watched the tent being erected—her paradise for the night—she remembered what he had said: *I have only one sleeping bag.*

Something warm unfurled inside her stomach and she glanced at her watch. Only a few more hours until dark. One tent. One sleeping bag. And a man whose touch made her hot.

She rose from the rock and walked away. She didn't even want to think what might happen.

"Bea." She heard him call her name, but she ignored it and kept walking. "Bea, where are you going?"

"Not far. Don't worry, I'll be back."

His first instinct was to go after her, but on second thought, he decided to stay. He'd already made a fool of himself over her more than once today. What was she to him? Nothing. Absolutely nothing.

He snapped a tent pole into place. If it hadn't been for her, he'd be far down the road now, heading for the West Coast, getting as far away from LaBelle as he could get. And then what? What would he do when he got to the Pacific? Catch a freighter? Keep on drifting?

He put the last tent pole into place, then reached for his handkerchief. Instead, he pulled out Bea's. Her fragrance still clung to the material. He pressed the damp square of linen to his nose and inhaled. The scent was sweet. He wondered if her body smelled like that. Did she put the scent of flowers in the crook of her elbows? Did she cover that tiny network of blue veins with the smells of spring?

"Dammit." He wadded the handkerchief into a tight ball and stuffed it back into his pocket.

If he had been near a gym, he'd have worked out. He'd have run until his legs were weak and his heart was pounding. He'd have battered a punching bag until his arms were sore. But he wasn't. He was trapped on Quachita Mountain with an impossible woman, a woman who smelled like spring.

Clenching his hands, he started after her. He had a good idea where she was.

Ten minutes later he discovered that he'd been right. That damned stubborn woman was standing at the bend in the road, tugging at a rock it would have taken two good-sized men to carry.

Without a word he went to help her. He'd learned the hard way that arguing with Bea Adams was useless.

* * *

By the time night came, they were both exhausted. They'd worked side by side on the pile of rocks, and still the road was blocked. They'd have to finish in the morning.

Perched on the front seat of his truck, they ate their meal in silence. Russ watched Bea out of the corner of his eye. She had smudges all over her face and hands. She'd broken the heel off one of her shoes, torn her skirt and ripped her blouse. Her hair was damp and mussed, and her legs were muddy to the knees. But she hadn't complained. Not once since they'd been trapped. In fact, once they'd started moving the rocks, she'd been downright cheerful.

Russ had never met a woman like her.

"You're staring," she said.

"Just thinking."

"About what?"

"You."

His honesty startled her. Usually the two of them resorted to word games or quips or even insults. She decided to be completely honest herself.

"I was thinking about you, too."

They studied each other. Neither wavered under the scrutiny.

"What were you thinking, Bea?"

"That you're a good man, Russ. A kind man."

"Don't pin any medals on me yet."

"Why?"

"The night is not over."

His eyes seemed to be saying things that he could not. They were intense and piercing, almost iridescent in the darkness of the truck. She looked away.

"You can rest easy," she finally said. "Even if one of us got any ideas, we're both too tired to do anything about it."

"Speak for yourself."

"You told me you no longer believed in love, Russ."

"I don't. But I believe in lust."

"Lust? For this?" Without thinking, she held one grubby leg up for inspection. "You must be joking."

"You don't know how sexy you are, do you, Tiger Lady?"

She hastily lowered her leg and smoothed her skirt down. "Don't call me that."

"You're like a tiger, sleek and beautiful and sensuous." He reached over and wiped a smudge from her cheek. "Even dangerous."

She was very still, daring not to show her turmoil with any quick moves. Let him keep his hands on her face, she thought. Let him think it didn't bother her.

"I guess lots of women like that line."

He traced her cheekbone with one finger. "Don't other men say those things to you, Bea? Don't they tell you how you make their hearts hammer and their breathing ragged?"

"No."

"Then they're fools."

"I don't date fools. I date sophisticated men."

"Fops and fools."

"You're a fine one to talk." Anger spotted her cheeks with color. She swatted his hand aside. "You, a drifter. A man who does nothing except ride a raggedy truck and listen to country music." She reached for the door handle. "How dare you make derogatory remarks about the men I date."

She jerked open the door.

"Going somewhere?"

"As far away from you as I can get." She clambered down from the truck.

He leaned out the door and called after her. "Be back in twenty minutes."

"I don't see any earthly reason why I should."

"Because that's when I'll have the bath water ready."

She stalked off into the dark. He'd just have to trust her guardian angel to watch after her. He didn't trust himself right now. For a few shaky moments, he'd almost pulled her into his arms. "That's what I get for taking up with Bea Adams in the first place," he muttered.

He'd known better. He'd stepped into the situation with his eyes wide open. And now he couldn't back out. He couldn't climb into his truck and drive off. Much as he wanted to put some distance between himself and Bea, he couldn't leave her stranded on the mountains.

"When we get to Memphis..." He realized he was talking out loud to himself, and his voice trailed off.

That's what he would do, wait until they got to Memphis, then help her rent a car and send her the rest of the way on her own. Forget about bargains and chivalry and fool talk of delivering her in one piece. He had to protect himself. What was there for him in Florence, Alabama, anyhow? For that matter, what was there for him at the end of any line?

Satisfied that he'd soon be on his way again—without Bea Adams—he got out of his truck and went to fetch wood for the fire and water for the bath. Her bath.

Bea was furious. The rain that had ravaged the mountain was nothing compared to the storm that was raging inside her. She kicked a rock with her good toe and stood still long enough to listen to it tumbling down the steep incline. She kicked another one. Behind her came the faint sound of whistling. Russ. He was back at the camp, no doubt proud of the way he'd infuriated her. What had he said he was going to do? She'd been so upset, she'd barely listened. Then she remembered. He was getting water for a bath. A bath! How was she going to take a bath on a mountain with a madman?

She sat on a rock, mindless of the of the cold and damp. Propping her chin in her hands, she looked out across the mountain. Chances were good there were all kinds of fearsome creatures lurking out there in the dark. But none of them could compare to Russ Hammond.

How had she managed to lose so much control? In Dallas, no matter what happened to her, she still felt as if she were at the helm of her ship, steering it clear of rocks and storms and pirates and anything else that would disrupt her steady course through the waters of life. Even when her boyfriends walked out on her, one by one, she still felt as if she were in charge of things.

But not with Russ. She hadn't been in charge of anything since she'd climbed aboard his pickup truck and rattle-banged her way into Pearcy, Arkansas.

Sitting on a rock on the mountain, she felt a million miles from home. She felt as if every familiar thing in her life had suddenly been sucked up in a giant vacuum cleaner, leaving her stranded without any point of reference. Her car was in Pearcy, her suitcase was in a tent on the side of a mountain, her job was in Dallas, her mother was in Florence, and her courage seemed to be on vacation.

She had no one except a blond, bearded giant with knowing blue eyes.

She looked up at the sky. It was sullen and heavy looking. She shook her fist at it.

"Don't you dare storm. Don't you *dare,*" she said, and then stalked back to camp.

Russ heard her coming before he saw her.

"You'd never make a stalker." He looked up as she came into the circle of his campfire.

"I don't plan to be a stalker." She moved close to the fire and held out her hands. "That feels good."

"Pull up a chair and sit down."

"A chair?"

"Campers always go prepared." He walked out of the circle of firelight and came back with a folding camp chair. He set it up with a flourish. "At your service, ma'am."

"This feels wonderful. I didn't know I was so tired." She sank back into the canvas, letting her body sag with the contours of the chair.

Russ felt all his protective instincts rush to the surface, and suddenly he was sorry that he'd be leaving her in Memphis. Not sorry enough to change his mind, but sorry enough to make amends before the fact. He decided to be extra nice to her during the time they had left together.

"I'm sorry for all the troubles you've had, Bea."

"I think you really mean that."

"I do." He unfolded another camp chair and sat down opposite her, watching her through the flickering flames. "You've been a trooper."

"So have you."

They watched each other in silence for a while. Finally, he spoke. "I'm sorry I made you angry a while ago."

"All these apologies . . . What has gotten into you?"

"I guess I'm feeling human."

"It's a pleasant change. How long can I expect it to last?"

He laughed.

"What's so funny?"

"You." He watched her in silence a while. Then, "You're not like other women, Bea."

"Thank you."

"I'm not sure I meant it as a compliment."

"I'll take it as one anyway."

They studied each other across the fire, like two mountain lions waiting to move in for the kill.

"Are you ready for a bath?" he asked suddenly.

"Is that a hint?"

"You *are* dirty."

"So are you."

"Under the right circumstances that could have been an offer."

"Then we should both be grateful these aren't the right circumstances." She stood up. "Which way to the showers?"

"Right in front of you."

She glanced down at the fire and saw a large dishpan filled with water. It was sitting on the edge of the coals, steaming.

"I don't believe it's big enough for two."

"We'll take turns. You can have the first bath."

"And what will you be doing?"

"Standing guard outside the camp."

"Guard against what? Mountain lions?"

"No. Myself." He disappeared into the tent and came back with a washcloth and a towel. "Better go ahead before the water gets too hot.'' He tossed the linens to her and stalked off into the night.

''Well, I'll be darned.'' Bea watched him until she could no longer see him. ''The man has scruples.''

She stood uncertainly for a while, not knowing where to start. She had never camped in her life, not even Girl Scout camp. Glory Ethel had urged her to join Girl Scouts the year Taylor had left, hoping, Bea supposed, that it would take her mind off things. But when she had discovered that all the Scouts had a camp out with fathers, she'd declined. What was the use of a camp out if you didn't have a father?

The night air was chilly, and she hugged herself, peering off into the darkness. She didn't hear a sound, not even a night bird. Where was Russ? Suppose he had walked out there and stumbled off the mountain in the dark? Or what if he had started walking and just kept on going? After all, he was a drifter. She guessed drifters would think nothing of leaving worthless old pickup trucks and helpless women behind.

Helpless women! Good grief, what was happening to her? One or two little setbacks and she was thinking of herself as helpless.

She snorted in disgust. There couldn't be much that was hard about camping out, otherwise droves of people would stay home rather than clog up the highways with their campers every summer.

She jerked up her washcloth and did the best she could with washing. When she finished, she rolled her muddy clothes into a bundle and dressed in a Victorian nightgown, white cotton, and her white terry robe. The clothes were warm and dry. Bea thanked her lucky stars for luggage that didn't leak.

"All finished," she called into the dark. There was no response, so she called again. "Russ? Are you out there?"

Still no answer. Her head felt light and her palms began to sweat as panic closed in on her.

"Russ?"

He came into the light, moving so silently she didn't hear him.

"I'm here, Tiger Lady." His eyes raked her from head to toe, but he didn't comment.

She felt vulnerable, and she didn't know why. That bothered her. She backed up behind the folding chair, clutching the damp canvas with tight, nervous fingers.

Russ stood on the other side of the firelight, so quiet and watchful he looked like a part of the mountain. The silence between them was as heavy as the cloud-burdened sky.

Bea wet her lips with her tongue.

"I guess it's your turn." Russ kept his silent vigil. She wet her lips again. "I'm sorry the water's so muddy."

"I've bathed in worse."

"I'll go stand guard...to fend off the mountain lions."

"No. It's too cold. And besides, I'm not going to let you go wandering around out there in the dark again.

"You're not going to *let* me!"

"That's what I said."

"If you think I'm going to stand here and watch—"

His roar of laughter interrupted her.

"If I'm that funny, maybe I should give up advertising and go into comedy."

"You're that funny, Tiger Lady. And stubborn and irritating and bossy, besides. I wouldn't put up with you for a minute if you weren't paying me handsomely."

"Just remember that." She had almost forgotten their bargain. For some silly reason she was sorry he'd reminded her. "I'm paying you."

He came around the fire and took her arm.

"Go into the tent, Bea. My sleeping bag is rolled out for you. There's a flashlight, and there are books in my duffle bag if you like to read."

"I'm not going to sleep in your bag."

"That's not an offer. That's an order."

"I never take orders. I give them."

"Dammit. This is no time to be stubborn. I'm sleeping on a pallet, you're sleeping in my bag, and that's that. Now, go inside so I can bathe." They glared at each other like two Roman gladiators before a fight to the death. Then his face softened. "Please."

"Since you beg so nicely..." She lifted the tent flap, then turned. "Russ, if you wouldn't try so hard to be a jackass, you'd be a very nice man."

"And if you wouldn't try so hard to be stubborn, you'd be a very nice lady."

She thought of saying something, then changed her mind. What else was there to say?

His bag was laid out, just as he'd said. She was too tired to fight any more. She rummaged into her suitcase and pulled out a dog-eared copy of *Gone With the Wind*. Taking Russ's flashlight, she settled back into the downy softness of his sleeping bag and began to read.

Outside, Russ began to whistle. She closed her mind to the sound. She didn't want to think of what he was doing out there, probably stripped naked, dripping water all over his magnificent chest.

Involuntarily, her eyes strayed toward the front of the tent. He was silhouetted against the firelight, his chest as naked as she had imagined, and just as broad.

She quickly turned her gaze back to her book. Nobody but Rhett Butler could take her mind off Russ Hammond.

As always, Rhett climbed straight into her heart. He was such a scalawag, such a renegade. Lord knows why a man like that appealed to her, but he did. She never read about Rhett Butler without thinking of Clark Gable. No other actor could possibly have played that part.

She smiled and ran her hands over the beloved print. Rhett Butler and Clark Gable. Neither one had ever broken her heart. Suddenly her hands stilled. Heroes in books and movies were safe. That's why she turned to them. That's why she preferred a good book or a good movie to a flesh-and-blood man.

It was something she'd never thought about, never until that moment. But then, she'd never been stranded on a mountain. The solitude of the mountain was conducive to introspective, analytical thinking.

Outside, Russ splashed water and hummed snatches of a song. Bea listened. Russ was a flesh-and-blood man. Every bit the scalawag, very much the renegade. Dangerously appealing. But not safe, not at all safe. *Real* men broke your heart. They took up with floozies and ran away. Just like Taylor Adams.

She didn't want to think about it anymore. She was tired. She pushed the book aside, snuggled down into the bag and shut her eyes.

Chapter Five

Russ lay on his pallet listening to the far-off call of a whippoorwill. On the other side of the tent, close enough to touch, Bea was sleeping, her chest rising and falling with her soft breathing. One arm rested on top of his sleeping bag, pale in the moonlight.

"Stubborn beauty," he whispered.

He lifted himself on his elbow so he could see her better. *Gone With the Wind* lay beside the pallet with Bea's hand still grasping it. *Romance.* She'd been reading romance. He smiled fondly into the darkness.

"You're a fraud, Tiger Lady."

Moonlight, streaming in from a crack in the tent flap, made a gleaming path across her cheek and down her bare arm.

He reached across the small space that separated them and touched her cheek with one finger. She didn't stir. Her skin was as soft as orange blossoms. And just as fragrant. In the confines of the tent, her scent wafted around him. He closed his eyes and inhaled deeply.

"Ahh, Bea. What have you done to me?"

She didn't move. Bolder now, he let his fingers drift over her cheek, touching her dark eyelashes, tracing the bridge of her nose, outlining the sensuous curve of her lips. She made a soft sighing sound, and her lips parted slightly. He pressed his finger against the moist warmth of her mouth. What would it be like to kiss that mouth? Just once?

His finger circled her lips again, ever so tenderly. She stirred, and for a moment he thought she would come awake.

He pulled his hand back and retreated to his pallet. Lonesomeness fell over him like a wet saddle blanket, weighing him down. He glanced over at Bea in the sleeping bag. If he could hold her close for a while, for just a little while, the lonesomeness might be divided and therefore bearable. At times like this, when the night was so quiet, he could have been the only person on the planet, he felt unfinished, as if God had started building him with bone and sinew and blood, and then had set him aside before he put all the parts in. Maybe the heart had been left out. Maybe that's why he'd never been able to find love. Maybe it had not been all his fault.

He rolled onto his side, turning his back to Bea, and closed his eyes. Things would be better when he got to Memphis.

Thunder rolled through the mountains like giant ninepins, and a great jagged spear of lightning tore through the dark skies.

Bea sat bolt upright, clutching her sleeping bag under her chin. Thunder roared through the mountains once more. She curved into herself and huddled down in the bag, holding her hands over her ears. Her world grew silent. Opening one eye, she peered around. The night was so black she couldn't see a thing, not a shadow, not a shape, not even a tiny pinpoint of light. For all she knew, she was totally alone. And lost. And scared.

She squinched her eyes shut. It was only a storm, she told herself. She would endure.

Lightning crackled once more, so close this time the hair on Bea's arms stood on end. She pressed her hands against her mouth to muffle her scream.

Russ came slowly out of his deep, dark slumber. Outside the tent, the elements were in turmoil. He heard the distant growl of thunder, complaining like a crotchety old man who had been disturbed from his nap. He wondered what had awakened him; he usually slept through storms.

He settled into his pallet, preparing to go back to sleep, when he heard the sound again, a soft whimper, like a puppy thrown into a muddy ditch on the side of the road.

"Bea?" He rolled over, squinting his eyes in the dark. He could see a dark shape on her side of tent. "Bea? Is that you?"

"Russ?"

Her head came up, and in another flash of lightning he could see her eyes, wide and scared. Sound and bright unnatural light filled the tent. Bea shuddered, and huddled down into her bedroll.

Russ was touched. Here was a woman who wanted all the world to know how independent she was, and yet she cried at romantic movies and cringed at thunderstorms. All of a sudden he felt strong and important and necessary.

He sat up and made room on his pallet.

"Would you like to come over here and sit with me awhile?"

"No." Her soft hair had covered the side of her face, like the broken wing of a bird, and she peered sideways at him through that curtain of black. "I'm doing just fine."

Another boom reverberated through the mountains. Bea jumped, then settled back into her covers, shivering.

"You know," he said, "I can't help but want a little bit of companionship at times like these. If you'd just sort of scoot over this way so we'd be close, I'd really appreciate it."

"You would?" She knew darned well that he was making it all up, and she never liked him as much as she did at that moment.

"I truly would." A flash of lightning illuminated his smile.

Without giving herself time to think too much about what she was doing, she scooted across the tent floor and onto his warm pallet. He took charge, arranging her so she was tucked under his arm with her head resting on his shoulder.

"There," he said. "That's better."

He felt her shiver as nature vented its wrath on the mountains. He started to talk then, for he guessed that what she was feeling was much akin to what he'd been feeling not so long ago—an intense lonesomeness that sometimes disguised itself as fear.

"When I was a little boy, not much more than four, I'd guess, my mother used to tell me stories every time it came a thunderstorm. My favorites were the ones about Christopher Robin and Winnie-the-Pooh."

"And the Hundred Acre Wood," Bea said. "I loved those stories, too."

"Did you sing the songs?"

"Yes. But not very well."

"I was marvelous."

He gave her a demonstration, his great rich voice wrapping about the simple, silly little words of the Winnie-the-Pooh songs until they weren't silly anymore, until they were words of great truth and wisdom. He sang of friendship and of how it always made the world seem a kinder, more forgiving place.

And soon Bea felt safe. Her head nodded and she went to sleep, resting on Russ's shoulder. Outside, the storm continued to lash the mountain.

Russ wrapped both arms around Bea and kissed the top of her head.

"Sleep well, my little Tiger Lady."

He stayed the way he was, sitting on the hard tent floor, his arms growing stiff around Bea's shoulder, thinking about his mother and the home he'd had when he had been four—green shutters at the windows and a white fence with roses that smelled good in the summertime. Strange that Bea should bring all that to mind.

As the storm abated, he thought of tucking her back into her sleeping bag on her side of the tent. But it felt good to be touching her. In the end he decided he would ease down onto his pallet and let her sleep there at his side.

"One night won't hurt." He slid downward, being careful not to wake her. "What can one night hurt?"

She sighed and cuddled close to him, settling against his side as if she belonged there. Russ had a sudden vision of how different his life could be, of coming home to logs burning in the fireplace and chicken stewing on the stove, of walking through the door and straight into the arms of a woman much like Bea. Not exactly, mind you. Someone sweeter, gentler. Perhaps someone who put Bea's fragrance on the blue-veined arch of her foot. Yes. Surely that.

If he were looking for a woman, he'd like a woman who smelled exactly like Bea. She reminded him of flowers in the springtime when the earth was green with promise.

Of course, he wasn't looking....

Bea stretched and wiggled herself awake.

At first she didn't know where she was. She snuggled down under her covers feeling warm and safe. Then slowly, ever so slowly, she became aware of the body next to her, a big muscular body radiating heat and giving off the friendly aroma of wool blankets and clean cotton T-shirts.

Russ. She gave a guilty start. She was piled all over him like whipped cream on a cake, her head burrowed into the warm curve where his arm joined his shoulder, one arm draped across his chest and one leg flung across his hips.

His hips, mind you. She carefully eased her leg off him. She felt hot all over with embarrassment. Waking in such a predicament didn't improve her temper one bit.

She had to get on her side of the tent—and fast. What if he woke up and found her draped all over him like a floozy? What would he think?

Suddenly he stretched and rolled, pinning her underneath him. His eyes flew open.

"Well, good morning." He smiled at her. "Did you sleep well?"

"It's hard to tell from this position. You're squashing my chest."

"Sorry." He rolled back over and propped his hands behind his head, smiling up at the canvas ceiling. "It's a remarkable day, don't you think?"

"What's so remarkable about it?" She scooted over to her side of the tent and tried to look seriously busy folding up her sleeping bag.

"Well... Here we are on this mountain with the morning sun out there shining down as if it didn't have anybody else to shine for except the two of us. Don't you find that remarkable?"

"I suppose...if you thought about it that way... hmm."

She couldn't bring herself to look him directly in the eye. Not after the way she'd been spread all over him this morning, like butter on toast. The thing that was so bad about it all was that she had actually enjoyed the feeling. *Enjoyed it,* mind you. And him a drifter. And likely to go no-telling-where at any minute without even giving her a backward glance or so much as a fare-thee-well.

Oh, he was terribly unsuitable and highly risky. She cursed her own judgment in starting such a journey with him. The very idea, going home, all the way to Florence, Alabama, with a man she hardly knew.

She supposed she'd been desperate when she made that decision. Yes, that was it. *Desperate.* And a little bit scared.

"Bea?"

"Hmm?" She slowly turned to face him.

His smile reminded her of baseball games in the summertime, sitting on the bleachers and cheering for the home team, of buttered popcorn in front of the fire with the family dog curled like a pretzel on the hearth, of two people in the kitchen, their hands sticky with dough, their fingers touching in the bowl as they made pizza crust together.

"Why don't you leave the sleeping bag rolled out?" he said. "I don't expect we'll be going anywhere today."

"Why not?"

"There's that big rock pile on the road, remember? It will take another day and a half to clear it out of the way."

"With me helping, the work will go faster."

She turned away from him so she wouldn't have to see his face. It reminded her of home.

"Hmm," he said, neither agreeing nor disagreeing. "Maybe."

He contemplated her back. Such a prideful, straight back she had. You wouldn't know to look at her now that she could feel so good cuddled up next to you at night, he thought.

Of course, he was going to leave her as soon as they got to Memphis. It would be better all the way around if he remembered that. No use getting sentimental over one night.

"Listen," he said. "Do you have anything in that suitcase besides skirts and high-heeled shoes?"

"A pair of slacks and some tennis shoes."

"Wear them. I'll get out of here and let you get dressed."

"Where will you go?"

"I'll scout around, see what this place looks like, gather some firewood so we can have hot coffee...." His voice trailed off. She looked so good in the morning, so fresh, her black eyes shining the way eyes on a woman ought to shine.

"Well...I'd best be getting on."

He left the tent quickly. Then when he got outside he wished he'd stayed. Just a minute longer. Just long enough to reach out and touch her hand, just long enough to make some kind of connection with her. It didn't feel right not to touch her this morning.

"Hell," he muttered. He'd left his jacket inside. Standing on the mountain with only his jeans and a T-shirt, he felt the chill of October.

Never mind. He wouldn't go back inside. Not yet. There was too much temptation inside that tent.

They spent all day trying to clear the rocks off the mountain road. Before they got started, they discussed going back down the mountain to a dirt side road Russ had spotted about a mile back, but they decided the rains would have made it impassable, and anyhow, they had no idea where it led. It would be best all around to press forward.

After that, neither of them talked much. For one thing, they were too busy working. For another, neither of them wanted the other to get the wrong idea. But they frequently sneaked glances when one of them thought the other wasn't looking.

Under the guise of wiping sweat off her face, Bea glanced at Russ from behind her hand. The day had turned hot, and he had taken off both his jacket and his T-shirt. The sun was slicking his skin and shining down on his blond hair, giving him a sort of halo.

Come to think of it, a halo wasn't such an inappropriate headpiece for him. After all, he'd rescued her more than once. Granted, he was the most maddening guardian angel anybody had ever heard of, but he was a guardian angel, nonetheless.

She tried not to need guardian angels. She didn't like the idea of being dependent on anybody. But she supposed once in her life she could be excused.

Last night she'd been weak, weaker than she'd ever been in her life. She clenched her fists and tilted her chin. Two more days. If she could get through two more days with Russ, she'd be home, home in Alabama, where the breezes were as soft as the speech patterns, home in Florence, where generations of Adamses and the rich red earth endured forever.

There she would find her strength.

She turned back to her work. She wouldn't think about what had happened. She'd just put it behind her and make sure it didn't happen again.

By the time nightfall came, they were both too tired to do much more than eat some of his canned rations and flop into the canvas chairs.

After supper Russ lifted his face toward the evening sky.

"It looks like it's going to be a beautiful night," he said. "Warm, balmy. Not like October at all."

"Just like October. It's always a capricious month."

"Like a woman."

"Women are not capricious."

"The ones I know are."

"I guess you've known the wrong women . . . up till now." She didn't know why she added that last part, but she had and it was too late to take it back.

Russ sat very still, looking at her in that watchful, expectant way of his. And then he smiled.

"Are you the right woman, Bea?"

"I'm the right woman for lots of things—for my ad agency, for my family, for my friends. Any way you look at it, I'm the right woman."

"Are you the right woman for me, Bea?"

"I didn't say I was."

"Yes, you did."

"Of course, I didn't."

"I heard you, plain as day."

"Then you misunderstood."

She stood up, stretching and yawning elaborately so he'd see how sleepy she was and stop talking to her.

"I guess it's time for us to turn in," he said.

He made it sound as if they were a team or worse yet, husband and wife, heading toward a four-poster with a feather mattress and a fuzzy blanket. In fact, he made the pair of them sound so inviting it scared her. *Imagine*. Her paired with a vagabond. *Ridiculous*.

Instead of answering him, she hurried inside the tent and got his sleeping bag. It was such a big bundle that she had some trouble negotiating back through the tent flap, but she managed.

"What are you doing?" he asked.

"I'm moving my sleeping bag."

"And where do you plan to move it to?"

"Oh, just someplace nice and breezy. It's too stuffy to sleep in a tent tonight."

"It will get colder later on."

"If I'm not mistaken, this bag is duck down."

He didn't answer her immediately. He was too angry, furious at her for wanting to move out and furious at himself for caring.

"You don't want to sleep on the ground," he finally said. "Something you don't want is liable to crawl in there with you."

Something she hadn't wanted had crawled in there with her last night, she thought. But she didn't say it aloud. Actually, he hadn't crawled in with her; she'd crawled in with him. And she'd liked it more than she cared to admit.

"I'll sleep in the truck. Nothing is going to crawl in with me in the truck."

He didn't say anything, merely tightened his jaw and watched her walk off toward the truck.

Damned stubborn woman. What did he care? He was going to leave her in Memphis anyhow.

Once Bea was headed toward his truck, she didn't look back. She hadn't meant to sleep in the truck; she had meant to spread her bag under that huge pine on the other side of their campfire. But she supposed sleeping in the truck wasn't such a bad idea. At least she wouldn't find herself curled around Russ Hammond in the morning—curled around him and *liking* it.

First she spread her bag in the cab and tried sleeping there. But she kept bumping her elbows on the steering wheel, and her feet kept getting tangled in the door handles.

Finally she got out and spread the bag in the truck bed. It was roomier, harder than the tent floor, but roomier, nonetheless.

She raised herself on her elbows and peered through the darkness toward the tent. She couldn't see a thing. She guessed Russ was inside on his pallet, sleeping like a baby, his big body warm and toasty, his chest rising and falling with reassuring regularity. Maybe he was even snoring a little. He had last night, she vaguely remembered. There was something comforting about a man lying beside you snoring, something appealing, something homey.

Sighing, Bea lay back on her hard bed. Finally she slept.

Russ lay on his pallet awhile, contemplating his situation. He was alone once more, but that was nothing new. The aggravating thing was that he didn't like it. He kept missing the smell of perfume in her hair and the soft kittenish way she fit against him when she slept.

Unable to sleep, he rummaged around in his duffle bag till he found a book; then he read for a while by the dim glow of his flashlight. But he couldn't concentrate. He kept thinking of Bea out there in his pickup truck.

Stubbornest woman alive. Once, in the middle of chapter four, he started to go out there and get her; then he decided against it. She might get a little cold later on, but she'd be all right. He guessed he would let her have her foolish way just this once.

With that settled, he put the book aside and slid under his covers.

While Bea and Russ slept, two men crept out of the dark, scrabbling their way over the rocks, passing a jug of moonshine back and forth.

"This ain't the way to travel, Hank."

Hank hitched his baggy overalls over his skinny frame and handed the jug to his cousin.

"Don't look at me, Bobbie Joe. I wadn't the one tore up the truck in that ditch back yonder."

Bobbie Joe hugged the jug to his fat stomach awhile, as if it were a woman; then he took a long swig and wiped his lips with the back of his hairless hand.

"Well, I wadn't the one wanted to set out at pitch-black dark."

"How else you gonna leave when ever'body in the county's after you?"

They were silent for a while, content to stumble along, fortified by liquor and anesthetized by ignorance. They didn't try to think of a way out of their situation. Planning ahead wasn't something they did.

Suddenly they came upon Russ's camp. Hank plucked Bobbie Joe's sleeve.

"Do you see what I see?"

"Yep. I ain't blind."

"Settin' there just as purty as a pitcher. Like it was waitin' for us."

"Yep. Just like God set it there so we wouldn't have to walk."

The two old men crept toward the pickup truck. They didn't consider what they were about to do was stealing; they considered that they had had a bit of good fortune and they would be foolish not to take advantage of it.

Bea came halfway awake.

I'm moving, she thought. And then decided she must be dreaming. That was it. She was too tired and she was having a bad dream.

She huddled back into her sleeping bag.

The truck hit a rut in the road, and Bea's head bounced on the hard floor. Jarred and astonished, she sat up. She *really* was moving. Russ's truck was banging along on some kind of side road, hitting ruts and rocks with little impartiality.

She pulled herself upright and leaned against the cab for balance.

"At least he could have had the decency to tell me he changed his mind." Wind stung her cheeks and chilled her ears. "Wait till I give that Russ Hammond a piece of my mind."

She tried to turn around and bang on the window, but the truck hit another big hole and she ended up crumpled in a heap, tangled in her sleeping bag.

"That man's going to hear from me." She struggled up onto her hands and knees.

Grabbing a handhold on the side of the truck bed, she banged on the window.

Inside the cab, Hank had charge of the wheel and Bobbie Joe had charge of the jug.

"Did you hear something, Bobbie Joe?" Hank asked as Bea smacked her palm against the glass behind their heads.

"Naw. Probably one of them old hoot owls settin' up a racket. They always carryin' on 'bout this time of night."

"It don't sound like no hoot owl to me. More like *whumpity, whumpity, whumpity.*"

They passed the jug between them, and Hank let go of the wheel long enough to take a big swallow. The truck somehow got itself down the road till Hank took over the driving again.

"Lissen." Hank cocked his head as Bea created another racket in the back end, banging and yelling for all she was worth.

"Stop this truck, Russ Hammond. Stop right this minute."

With Bobbie Joe hunched over to one side, bent over his jug and the night as black as shoe polish and the sleeping bag flapping up in her face from the wind, Bea could barely make out one head and one set of shoulders in the cab.

"I'm going to really scream if you don't stop, Russ," she yelled from the back, her voice borne away by the wind.

The sound came to Hank as a faint moaning, the kind ghosts might make.

"I think somebody's in this truck with us, Bobbie Joe."

"That liquor's done gone to your head. Ain't nobody settin' here but the two of us, and you so ugly you don't count."

"Lissen... Don't you hear that? *Whooo, whooo.* Like spooks and haints."

"The Devil's drawers! Stop this truck and let me drive. I ain't about to go down this mountain with a crazy man at the wheel."

Hank pulled the truck off the road, careless of tail pipes and such, dragging over rocks and jouncing through ruts until he had come to a bone-jarring stop.

Bea rolled around, bruising parts of her body she didn't even know she had, and finally ended up sitting in the middle of the truck bed with the sleeping bag draped over her head.

About the time she was clawing her way out of the bag, Hank and Bobbie Joe rounded separate corners of the truck.

"Oh, Lordee, oh, Lordee, oh, Lordee. It's a haint from hell," Hank screamed. "I confess. I done it. I done it. Jest don't send me to eternal damnation."

Bea froze. The sleeping bag settled slowly back over her head.

Dear merciful heavens, she thought. *I've been kidnapped.*

Chapter Six

"Shut up, you old fool," Bobbie Joe yelled at his companion. "Haints don't wear sleeping bags."

He reached over and plucked at the sleeping bag. "Come out, come out," he chanted, "whoever you are."

Good grief, Bea thought. There were two of them. Two kidnappers reeking of corn liquor and talking about *haints*. Just wait till she got her hands on that Russ Hammond. She'd kill him.

But first she had to deal with her kidnappers.

She rose up tall and strong under the bag, then flapping her arms for effect, she screeched, "Boo-oo-ooo."

Hank nearly jumped off the mountain. "I *told you* it was a ghost, Bobbie Joe," he whined.

"You gonna make me lose my religion, Hank," Bobbie Joe said as he clambered over the side of the truck.

Bea could hear him coming. She braced herself for the attack. She was headed home and *nothing* was going to stand in her way.

Bobbie Joe jerked the bag and Bea swung her fist at the same time. Her fist propelled the bag Bobbie Joe's way. The fist did no damage, but the bag was lethal. Both of them got tangled up and landed in a heap on the truck bed.

"Hell, there's a she-cat in this darned bag," Bobbie Joe said.

"Get your hands off me," Bea yelled. As she scrambled upright, her arms and legs were both going like windmills, but much to her disgust, the bag kept getting between her and her target. "Let go of me, you sawed-off little runt."

"Who you callin' a sawed-off little runt?" Bobbie Joe took time off from battle to give her an offended look.

His pride was his downfall.

One of Bea's legs was finally free of the bag, and she caught him in the stomach with a whacking roundhouse kick. He wheezed once or twice, and then he folded in the middle like a beanbag that had lost all its stuffing.

Having recovered from his encounter with haints, Hank joined the fray. Before Bea had time to savor her victory, he was over the side of the truck, his bony hands jerking her arms behind her back. With his teeth, he pulled a length of rope out of the tobacco pocket of his overalls and trussed her up like a calf ready for the market.

Hank dusted his hands together, proud of himself, and glared down at his fallen companion.

"Now who you callin' an old fool?"

"Both of you," Bea said. They had tied her arms and legs but had forgotten her mouth. "Just who do you think you are, stealing a truck and kidnapping a woman? Don't you know that's against the law?"

"Where's the law?" Hank stood spreadlegged in the center of the truck bed, looking drunk and lopsided. "I don't see no law. Do you, Bobbie Joe?"

Bobbie Joe groaned and lifted his head. When he saw the she-cat tied up, he got some of his spirit back.

"You durned tootin' they ain't no law around here."

"Just wait till my friend finishes with you," Bea said.

She crossed her fingers, which were already behind her back, much to her mortification. A fine pickle she was in. But she was too angry to be scared. And much too busy. Her mind was as busy as Christmas elves trying to think of a way out of her predicament. If she couldn't outwit two old drunk mountaineers, then she was losing her touch.

"What friend?" Hank twisted his head this way and that, nearly losing his balance in the process. "I don't see no friend, do you, Bobbie Joe?"

"You will," Bea said, not giving Bobbie Joe time to gather his wits—if he had any in the first place. "When he gets here, you'll wish I'd called the law instead."

She sent a silent prayer winging upward that Russ would wake up, hoping he would come after her and wishing to goodness that he'd hurry up. Both Bobbie Joe and Hank were silent, watching her with the curiosity of children over a strange new toy. She seized her advantage and continued talking, inventing as she went.

"He's bigger than this mountain and meaner than two wildcats put together. When he gets mad, he goes crazy... and he's really going to be mad when he sees what you've done to me. If I were you, I'd cut these ropes and let me go before he gets here."

Bobbie Joe was tired of listening to her, so he stuffed a handkerchief in her mouth. All he'd meant to do was borrow a truck so he wouldn't have to walk. He hadn't counted on ending up with a talkety woman. And Lord, could she talk. He'd gotten a headache listening to her. Maybe the best thing would be to cut her loose. Of course, he wanted to be out of the way when they did. She had a kick like a jug of moonshine.

"I don't know 'bout lettin' you go," he said, glancing at his companion for guidance. "What do you think, Hank?"

"Well . . ." Hank cocked his head this way and that, looking at Bea from all angles. There was bound to be some use for her. He didn't much care about home cooking anymore, preferring the convenience of canned pork and beans, and he didn't have anyplace of his own to keep clean, and he had lost his appetite for women some years back. Still, she'd been dropped into his lap for some purpose. He just couldn't think what that purpose was.

"I got it. I got it!" Bobbie Joe suddenly yelled. "We'll sell her."

Russ came awake with the unsettling feeling that something was wrong.

He rolled up on his elbows and squinted into the darkness. There was nothing to see except a pale sliver of moonlight coming through a crack in the tent flap. He started to settle back onto his pallet, but that strange feeling of something amiss made the back of his neck prickle.

"Stubborn woman, out there in the pickup." He got out of his pallet. "If I don't check on her, I never will go back to sleep."

Yawning and stretching his stiff muscles, he made his way out of the tent. The night was black, with only a pale excuse of a moon showing behind some clouds. Russ looked across the campfire and saw empty space where his truck used to be.

He rubbed his hands over his eyes and looked again. Nothing was there.

"Dammit. What has that woman done now?"

He strode across the camp and stood looking down the mountain.

"If that's not just like her to go off and leave me stranded here."

Anger clouded his reason for a moment; then a bit of sanity returned. It was not like Bea at all. She was anything but impulsive. Stubborn, yes. Maddening, definitely. Self-reliant, for sure. But would she take off in the middle of the night, leaving her clothes behind, without a word to him?

The same uneasy feeling that had awakened him returned full force. Dropping to his knees, he scanned the ground. It was still muddy from the recent storm, and it was covered with tracks, large tracks made by the heavy kind of shoe a man might wear to plow the fields.

Russ's heart slammed hard against his ribs, and he had to breathe deeply in order to get air into his lungs. Someone had taken his truck. And where was Bea?

"Bea!" He stood up, cupping his hands around his mouth. "Bea! Bea!" His voice echoed through the mountains and bounced back to him, a faint, lonesome sound.

Fighting panic, he raced to the tent and grabbed his jacket and his flashlight. Then he combed the area around the campsite, looking for Bea, alternately hoping to find her and praying he would not, praying that he was wrong about the tracks, praying that she had gotten into the truck and driven serenely down the mountain.

All sorts of visions came into his mind: Bea, lying unconscious behind a rock, her clothing torn and her face pressed into the mud. Bea, still and white, her eyes staring sightlessly up at the moon. Bea...

"Stop it."

He forced the visions out of his mind and continued his search, cursing the darkness that hampered him. He turned his flashlight behind every rock and tree around the camp. Bea was nowhere to be found.

Finally he went back to the site where his truck had been and knelt down to study the tracks. He was no tracker, but it appeared to him that they only led up to the truck and not away. Suppose the men in the brogans had taken Bea with them? Horrible thought.

Standing once more, he trained his flashlight onto the ground. Tire tracks clearly marked where the truck had turned and headed back down the mountain.

There was nothing to do but follow the truck. Russ set out on foot.

It was nearly dawn by the time he found Bea.

First he heard the voices. He followed the sound, easing along quietly through the trees until he came upon two old men sitting on rocks in front of a small campfire, quarreling loudly and drunkenly.

"I say we sell her."

"And I say where the hell at?"

Russ took cover behind a huge oak tree and surveyed the area. His truck was parked nearby, its bed backed toward the fire. Bea Adams sat in the middle of the truck, bedraggled and dirty, very much alive and as mad as a dozen fighting tomcats.

Thank God, Russ said to himself. He studied her in the pale pinkish light of dawn. She appeared to be unharmed, but her feet and legs were trussed with a rope and a dirty handkerchief was tied around her mouth.

He turned his attention back to the men. One of them was the shape and color of a turnip, his round belly bulging against his overalls and his face blotched purple with too much sun and too much liquor. There was very little hair on his head, or anywhere else, as far as Russ could tell. His hands and the portion of his arms showing below his shirtsleeves were hairless.

His companion looked like all the fat had been siphoned off him, leaving a saggy old skin to cover his bones. His hair stuck out in puffs of gray, with huge shiny bald spots showing here and there, as if somebody had done a poor job of plucking him.

Both of them were very old men, and apparently deep in their cups. A jug lay on its side by the fat one. As far as Russ could tell, neither of them had a weapon of any kind.

He could probably go in and overpower both of them without any trouble, but he decided to wait and watch. When he knew his opponents, *then* he would make his move.

"Look at her, settin' over there," the skinny man said, "meaner'n a rattlesnake."

"Well, I wadn't the one who said let's turn her hands loose and git a little circulation."

"She durned near scratched my eyes out."

The skinny old man had long scratches down the side of his face, and the fat one didn't look as if he had fared any better: two angry red welts rose on his hairless arms and his right ear looked as if somebody had tried to twist it off and nearly succeeded.

Russ grinned. Bea must have put up a heck of a fight.

"I *still* say we ought to sell her." The fat one was talking again.

"Who'd want her? Ain't nobody wants a woman skinny as that. She ain't got hardly no flesh on her bones."

"Well, what we gonna do with her, Hank? I ain't fixin' to set her loose. If she didn't kill us first, she'd have the law on us quick as you could say *scat*."

The law? Russ bent around the tree for another look. They didn't appear to be hardened criminals, but if he'd learned anything these last few days, he'd learned not to judge by appearances.

"Shoot, I tole you them two old chickens wadn't worth takin', but you said, 'Yeah, we'll git us a rooster and be in the chicken bidness.' That's what you said, Bobbie Joe, and I lissened to you like a old fool."

Hank hunkered over his knobby old knees, looking forlorn, and Bobbie Joe stared into the fire, apparently looking for a way out.

Russ decided to provide it.

"Good evening, gentlemen," he said as he stepped from behind the tree and stood posing. He wanted to impress upon them that he was big and strong and fully capable of whipping them both and leaving them in a pile. "Don't bother to get up. I'll join you."

Bea had never been so glad to see anybody in her entire life. She called his name, but it came out a pitiful muffled sound against her gag. He glanced in her direction and shook his head. The movement was so slight she wasn't certain if she'd seen it. Then he sat down on a good-sized rock beside her kidnappers.

"Looks like you've been having a party." Russ nodded toward the overturned jug.

"Who the devil are you?" The skinny one was talking, the one called Hank.

"Fool," Bobbie Joe interrupted. "Don't you figure he was settin' in that tent where we done took the truck?"

"That's a clever deduction, gentlemen." Russ smiled at Bobbie Joe; then he turned and nodded toward Bea. "And I see you've been kind enough to take the little woman off my hands."

"Shoot, we didn't mean to," Bobbie Joe said.

"Nobody in his right mind would," Russ agreed. "She's a regular rattlesnake...and too skinny besides."

"That's jest what I said, I said she's meaner than a rattlesnake. Ain't that what I said, Bobbie Joe?"

"I couldn't agree more, gentlemen. How much would you pay me to take her off your hands?"

Bea figured that when she got over being mad at Russ, she'd admire his cleverness.

Hank and Bobbie Joe scratched their heads and looked at each other. Then both of them began to fumble in the pockets of their overalls.

"I ain't got nothin' but a twenny." Hank held up the wrinkled bill. "How 'bout you, Bobbie Joe?"

"Looks like it comes to exactly seven dollars point ought six." He spread a five and two ones on the ground, then lined the six pennies up beside the bills.

"I don't know if that's enough." Russ shook his head. "She's a powerful lot of trouble."

Bea decided that he was enjoying himself far too much.

"Then there's the matter of my truck," Russ added. "I didn't expect to have to spend most of the night searching for my truck."

"We wadn't gonna go far," Hank said. "Jest over to the next county till the stink died down about them chickens."

Bobbie Joe nodded his head vigorously.

Russ actually began to feel sorry for them.

"I'll tell you what," he said, scooping up their money. "I'll consider this a downpayment for relieving you of the woman. You can work off the rest."

"What kind of work?" Hank asked.

"If you'll come with me, gentlemen, I'll show you." Russ led the way to the pickup. "But first I have to deal with the little woman."

He climbed into the back and untied her. Then he picked her up and held her hard against his heart for a moment.

"This is all your fault," she said.

"For a woman who is worth only twenty-seven dollars and six cents, you talk too much." Russ's eyes twinkled as he smiled down at her.

"I'll get you, Russ Hammond."

"I'm sure you will." Russ climbed down with Bea and turned to the hapless kidnappers. "Hop into the back, gentlemen. We're going for a ride."

Inside the cab, Bea sagged against the seat.

"I thought you would never come."

"I thought I would never find you."

Russ put the truck into gear and started back to camp just as the sun spread its light over the mountain.

"They didn't hurt you, did they, Bea?" His expression was anxious, and there were dark circles under his eyes from too little sleep.

"No. I'm a little bruised from bumping around in the back end, but I'm unharmed."

The anxiety that had kept Russ going suddenly drained away, and in its place came anger.

"You should never have been out there in the truck in the first place."

Her own anger flared to match his.

"I wouldn't have if it weren't for you."

"I wanted you in the tent, as I recall."

"Under your covers."

"That was because of the storm."

"Well, the storm was over when I woke up in your arms."

"Did you leave the tent because you didn't like being in my arms . . . or because you did?"

She didn't say anything. She wasn't about to admit that he was right about everything. Besides, she was too tired to argue.

She sank low in her seat and propped her head in her hands.

"It looks as if I'll never get home."

Russ's anger died as quickly as it had sprung to life. He stretched his hand across the seat and placed it on Bea's shoulder.

"I'm sorry, Bea . . . for everything."

She turned so she could look at him. His face was gentle with feeling, and at that moment she thought he must be the kindest man in all the world.

"So am I," she whispered. Then she shut her eyes.

By the time they got back to camp, she was sound asleep. Russ tenderly lifted her down. Holding her in his arms, he faced her captors.

"Wait here, gentlemen. I'll be right back."

He carried Bea inside the tent and tucked her into his pallet. She sighed softly and burrowed under the covers.

"Stubborn woman," he whispered, smoothing her hair back from her face. "You're worth more than twenty-seven dollars—far, far more."

He kissed the blue-veined skin inside her wrists, then pulled the covers close under her chin and left the tent.

Hank and Bobbie Joe were waiting for him. He led them around the curve in the road to the rockslide. It took the three of them only two hours to clear away the rest of the rocks.

Bea heard them come back to camp. Their voices drifted through her consciousness, weaving in and out of her slumber until she came fully awake. She sat in the tent, listening . . . and smiling.

"It ain't right somehow, Russ," Hank said, "you givin' us back our money and payin' us for that work besides. Not after all we done."

"Naw," Bobbie Joe added. "It don't seem fittin'."

"Take it." Bea could see Russ through the tent flap, pressing money into their hands. "Go back home, pay your neighbors for those two chickens, and then don't get into any more trouble."

"You must be some kind 'a saint." Hank stuffed his share of the money into his overalls.

"Yeah, especially livin' with that she-cat." Bobbie Joe pulled a snuff box out of his pocket and put his money inside. "You have our sympathies."

"So long." Russ waved them goodbye, then went inside the tent.

Bea was sitting on his pallet, disheveled and sleepy-looking, her white gown ripped on the sleeve and her eyes smudged with dark circles and a good portion of mountain mud. He'd never seen a more beautiful sight in all his life. Having her alive and smiling brought a lump to his throat.

Hanging half in and half out of the tent, he swallowed discretely. "You're awake," he said, still holding onto the tent flap. "How do you feel?"

"Like a she-cat."

"You heard?"

"I did. And do you know what I think, Russ Hammond? I think you're a big, old, softhearted fraud."

For some reason, he liked that. It pleased him that Bea thought of him as having a heart, particularly a soft heart. He came into the tent, smiling.

"You have mud all over your face, Bea." Reaching out, he wiped a smudge on her cheek. She felt the way a big-eyed woman ought to feel, like babies and rose petals and warm winter blankets all rolled up in one.

Long after the smudge was gone, his hand lingered on her face.

"Russ?"

"Ummmh?"

Their gazes got tangled up and their breath mingled as they sat side by side, pleased yet watchful.

This will never do, Bea thought.

How can I ever leave her? he wondered.

But he had to, he had to leave her soon, before his heart reached out for her, before it reached out and got such a tight hold he would never want to let her go.

"It's time to leave." He became brusque. "I'll give you five minutes to be ready to hit the road."

"The road is clear?"

"Yes. I'm taking you home."

He left the tent quickly and began to dismantle the camp.

Bea made quick work of dressing. She would clean the mud off later. She was going home, home to Glory Ethel and Jedidiah and Samuel and Molly, home to the Victorian house in Florence, Alabama, a house with wide rooms and high ceilings and sweet-smelling sheets, a house with a brass bed instead of a sleeping bag . . . a house without Russ Hammond.

Her fingers stilled on her buttons. Home without Russ? A sadness weighed down on her, and her steps dragged as she left the tent.

"I'm ready."

Even her voice reflected her sadness. She hoped he thought she was just tired.

"Good. The sooner we leave the mountain, the better."

That made her sad, too, that he seemed eager to leave the mountain. She remembered how they had sat in the truck, cozy and dry with the rain beating the windows, how they had laughed and joked. She remembered how she had felt, waking up in his arms, warm and contented, at peace with the world.

She felt almost as if she were *leaving* home instead of going home. *How silly.*

He dismantled the tent, she took one last look at the mountain, and then she climbed into the truck.

Russ started the vehicle without much coaxing, and soon they were on the road again, riding side by side, the wind whistling around the ill-fitting windows and Willie Nelson wailing in their ears.

Bea hardly noticed the music. She hardly noticed anything except the set of Russ's jaw and the intense way he drove, as if he couldn't wait to be rid of her. She tried to start a conversation, but his reply was so curt she decided to keep silent.

Within two hours they were off the mountain and on the superhighway. Before long, they had found a place to eat, one of those little frame restaurants with checked gingham curtains in the window and a hog-shaped sign in the yard, Eat Here.

They did. They ordered a meal and ate with a minimum of conversation.

"Do you want more bread?" Bea asked at one point.

"Please."

Much later Russ said, "Would you pass the pepper?"

She handed it across the table, being careful not to make contact with his hand.

"Thank you."

"You're welcome."

It was a relief to leave the steamy closeness of the restaurant and climb into the rusty old truck. Even the country music was a relief, Bea decided as they rattled down the road. At least it was something. At least it was noise to cover the awkward pauses and the loaded glances and the screaming silences.

The rhythm of the tires and the plaintive crooning of the blues lulled Bea. She dozed.

Russ glanced over at her from time to time, drinking her in. Now that she was sleeping, he felt at ease studying her. She really wasn't beautiful in a traditional way. Her eyes were too big and her skin was too pale and she was a little on the thin side. He guessed it must be her spirit that made him think she was the most glorious woman he'd ever met.

That scared him. He didn't know when he'd started thinking of her in that way. He didn't even want to know.

He was leaving her . . . before she left him.

It was inevitable, of course. She was a well-to-do, successful woman, accustomed to the finer things in life. And what did he have to offer? An old beat-up truck, a battered suitcase and a pair of snakeskin boots. That about summed up his worth. A woman like her wouldn't stay with him a minute, let alone a lifetime.

He glanced out the window. The road sign said only sixteen more miles to Memphis.

His heart felt heavy. It was nearly dark, but they should still be able to find a rental-car agency open. He wouldn't take her money, of course. He'd even offer to pay for her rental car.

She'd be glad to be rid of him. It would be best all the way around—for both of them.

The miles whizzed by, faster and faster. Only twelve miles to Memphis. Then ten.

He didn't feel right, somehow. Perhaps if he explained a little before he told her goodbye. He cleared another lump from his throat and began to speak. "It happened in Florida."

The sound of Russ's voice brought Bea wide awake. She jerked her head upright and glanced out the window. A road sign proclaimed eight more miles to Memphis.

"What happened in Florida?" She yawned and rubbed her eyes, then turned to face him.

"LaBelle, Florida." He didn't glance her way. His profile was set and still, and his eyes looked as if they were focused on something she couldn't see. "I had a citrus grove down there. In the early spring it smelled so sweet..." He stared out the window, silent now.

She waited. A light rain began to fall. Russ turned on the wipers, and their blades began a soft swishing rhythm against the windows.

He was silent for so long, she feared he had changed his mind. Then suddenly he started talking again.

"I loved everything about that state, the sky was so blue it sometimes hurt your eyes to look at it, the sunshine—always the sunshine—so warm you didn't have to wear clothes." He laughed, but it was not a sound of mirth. "I had a private lake. We loved to cavort naked. Just the two of us...

"I thought it would last forever," he added after a brief pause. "Wasn't that crazy, to think something could last forever?"

He turned then and looked at her. Even in the waning light, Bea could see the question in his eyes, as if he wanted her to argue with him, to say, "Of course, it wasn't crazy. Things *do* last forever."

But she wouldn't tell him lies. She knew nothing lasted forever. Not Taylor and not a string of men who had pledged more than friendship.

Instead of lying, she asked a direct question. She was more than curious about this man who was her rescuer, her knight in python boots and a ramshackle pickup truck. "What didn't last forever, Russ?"

"My marriage."

"Your marriage?" Bea squeezed the handle of her purse so hard her knuckles went white. Anger made her see spots in front of her eyes. "You have a wife?"

"Had. Past tense. Lurlene two-timed me with the B-Quick Man." He laughed and became almost jocular. Telling Bea about Lurlene had released something inside him, unlocked some secret door that he hadn't even known he'd kept locked. "It was no love match from the beginning. More like a marriage of convenience. But we both said the vows and meant them . . . till death do us part. I guess she should have said, 'till the B-Quick Man do us part.'"

Relieved, and guilty because she was feeling that way, Bea reached across the seat and squeezed his arm.

"I'm sorry, Russ. That must have hurt."

"No. It just taught me what I knew all along. I'm a rambling man and always will be. There's no use thinking any other way. I guess I'd have left her sooner or later."

He turned but couldn't see Bea's face in the dark, couldn't tell how she was taking his deliberate lie.

God in Heaven, he prayed silently, *if you can hear me up there, forgive me for what I am about to do.*

"Most men do," Bea agreed. Then she slumped down in her seat and stared out the window. "They all leave sooner or later."

She sounded so forlorn, Russ felt the urge to pull her across the seat and tuck her under his arm and rub her tense shoulders and sing a silly song just to bring a smile to her face. That was ridiculous, of course. She wasn't his worry.

Anyhow, they'd be in Memphis as soon as they crossed the bridge.

Chapter Seven

Up ahead, the truck lights illuminated the Arkansas-Memphis Bridge.

Russ and Bea both looked straight ahead, as if the bridge had a major significance for them, as if crossing the river would mean more than moving from one state to the next, from Arkansas to Tennessee, as if it would mean they had left something of themselves behind and couldn't bear to think what they would do without it.

The rhythm of the windshield wipers and the sing-song of the tires on wet pavement lulled them both into thinking they might drive forever, the bridge might not end in Memphis but go on into eternity, with the two of them sitting side by side looking out the window.

On the radio Hank Williams, Jr. was wailing another lonesome song about the heartbreak of being left behind. For the first time in her life, Bea found some appeal in country music. It spoke directly to the way she was feeling.

They rode in silence until they came to the bridge.

Russ couldn't put off telling her any longer. He turned the radio down and eased up on the accelerator so the bridge would last longer.

"Bea?"

Something about the question in his voice made her head snap back. He was usually telling, not asking.

"Yes?" She turned to see his face, but it was in profile, the nose straight and chiseled and the beard glowing in the city lights that had suddenly sprung out of the darkness.

He opened his mouth to say, *I'm going to leave you in Memphis, let you drive home in a rental car, and I'll be on my way.* But before the first word was out of his mouth, he came upon an ancient car, sideways in his lane, the red taillights winking crooked looking into the night.

"What the..." He rammed on his brakes, then fought to keep his truck from skidding on the wet pavement.

The cars behind him merely pulled into the passing lane and went on their way, the drivers turning their faces straight ahead, not wanting to get involved.

"What in the world's going on?" Bea asked, straining forward to see.

"It looks like they've skidded halfway off the bridge."

Russ put on his emergency blinkers and pulled as far out of the lane as he could.

"Wait right here, Bea. I'll see what's happening."

His hand was on the door handle before she spoke.

"Russ..." She reached over and caught hold of his sleeve. "Be careful."

"Thanks, Bea."

He climbed out of the truck, feeling good, as if somebody had just informed him he'd won an award of some kind. He walked toward the car, peering through the darkness to see who was inside. Two gray heads were pressed close together in the front seat, and a big yellow cat stared at him from the back window.

Russ walked around the red taillights and approached the front of the car. Its right wheel was hanging off the bridge, giving the whole vehicle a precarious tilt. The front fender was crumpled where it had slammed into the guard rail.

Russ leaned down and tapped on the window. The two old people on the front seat stared staunchly ahead. He tapped again, louder this time. Except for a slight shiver, the old couple seemed not have heard him.

Cupping his hand around his mouth, he yelled at the window, "I'm Russ Hammond, and I'm going to help you."

Still no response. He thought about carefully opening the front door and getting the people out, but he didn't want anything to scare them.

He tried to talk to them once more.

"Don't be afraid. If you'll come out of the car, I'll pull it back onto the bridge."

The old man slowly turned his head. He studied Russ for a long while, and then, seeming to find him satisfactory, leaned over and cranked down the window.

"Mama won't leave the cat," he said.

"We'll get the cat out, too. Just let me help you from the car."

The two old people bent their heads together once more, whispering. The old man then turned back to Russ. "Mama says no."

With that, he put his arm around his companion and stared out the front window. Russ didn't know what to do. He couldn't leave them there and hope someone else would come along to pull them back onto the bridge. And he couldn't seem to make them understand what needed to be done.

He leaned into the window and spoke earnestly to them.

"Wait right here," he said, as if he expected them to go somewhere. There didn't seem much chance of that. In fact, he doubted that anything less than an act of God would move them out of that car.

He sprinted back to the truck and climbed in beside Bea.

"What's happening out there?"

"You're not going to believe this. That car is poised to tilt into the river, and the two old folks in it refuse to budge. The old man says *Mama* won't leave her cat."

"Maybe I can help."

"It's worth a try."

Bea and Russ went back to the front of the car, and Bea leaned into the window. "Hi. I'm Beatrice Adams."

The old man slowly swiveled his head like a turtle peeping out of its shell. His scrawny neck was grooved and furrowed with age, and his eyes were watery and red-rimmed. Bea smiled at him.

"Good evening, Miss Bea." He nodded formally, as if he were greeting her at the Governor's Ball. "I'm Macon Grimes and this is my wife, Ophie." He patted his wife's wrinkled hand. "Say hello to Miss Adams, Ophie."

Ophie smiled shyly, then ducked her head and whispered, "Hello."

"It's her cat, you see," Macon explained. "Miss Roosevelt back there is about to have kittens, and we don't want to upset her by leaving the car."

"Oh, the poor little kittens," Miss Ophie said.

"I certainly understand, and I want to help the kittens, too." Bea reached back until she felt Russ's arm, then she caught hold. "Will you excuse us, Mr. Grimes? I'm going to talk to Mr. Hammond about your problem and see what we can do."

"Certainly, my dear." Macon and Ophie leaned their heads together and began to whisper.

Bea held on to Russ's arm all the way back to the truck. Somehow, holding on to him was both comforting and reassuring, as if he were a great shield between her and anything that might bring her harm. She supposed that being alone with him in the mountains must have caused a strange kind of bonding. It would probably vanish once she got home, but for the moment, she enjoyed it.

He helped her into the truck, and squeezed her hand while they talked. He might not have been aware of what he was doing, but that was all right with Bea. Just having him there, touching her, made all the difference.

"I think I can talk them into coming out," Bea said.

"How?"

"I'll make a nest for the cat using one of your blankets, and then I'll get into the car—"

"No!"

"What do you mean, no?"

"I will not let you get into a car that's hanging over the Mississippi River."

She jutted out her stubborn chin. "You won't *let* me?"

"You're damned right I won't."

She scooted away from him, and they sat on opposite sides of the truck glaring at each other. The sweet
nostalgia of a coming to a journey's end vanished in the
face of their anger.

No fury burned brighter than that of a man whose
passions had been too-long denied. He wanted her, Russ
admitted that to himself. Right now. Sitting on a bridge
in the rain and in the dark, he wanted Bea Adams. He
was furious with himself...and with her. Dammit, why
couldn't life be simple? Why couldn't he have driven
across the bridge without stopping and left Bea at a
rental-car agency? Then he would be rid of her. He
wouldn't have to worry any more about her broken car
and her sore toe and her bad dreams and her kidnapping and now, for Pete's sake, about her fool notion of
getting into a car that was about to topple off the
bridge.

"Dammit all, Bea...." Russ ran his hand through his
hair. "If I weren't around to take care of you, there's no
telling what would happen."

"I managed quite nicely for a good many years without you."

"I don't know how.... Dammit!" He banged his fist
against the dashboard. There was no way he could leave
Bea now, not until he got her safely to Florence—which
could be sometime around Christmas at the rate they
were going.

"Grab one of my blankets out of my duffle bag and
follow me," he said as he climbed down from the truck.
Then, looking over his shoulder at her, he added, "And
don't argue."

"Why would I possibly waste my breath that way?
Talking to you is like talking to a post oak."

Russ didn't hear her; he had already gone back to the lopsided vehicle. Sighing, Bea did as she was told.

By all that was right and proper, she should hate Russ Hammond. He'd done nothing for the last few days except order her around—nothing except hauling her car into Pearcy, getting soaking wet retrieving her suitcases, shielding her from bad dreams and rescuing her from kidnappers.

With her hands in his duffle bag, she grew still. Most men would have abandoned her rather than go to all that trouble. But not Russ. He'd stuck by her. Cheerfully, most of the time. She had never known such men existed—except her brother, of course, and he didn't count.

By the time she got to the car, Macon and Ophie were standing outside and Russ was climbing gingerly into the back seat.

Bea thought her heart would stop. What if that car tumbled into the river? He was a big man. What if his weight was just what it took to tip the vehicle into the cold waters of the Mississippi?

"Russ!" She hurried to him, bending over to watch anxiously as he settled onto the back seat with the cat.

"Be still, Bea. Don't make any sudden moves," he cautioned, never taking his eyes off the cat.

Miss Roosevelt was up against the door, her back arched and her claws bared.

Oh, Lord, Bea thought. *If he doesn't fall into the river, he'll be clawed to pieces.*

"Be careful," she whispered.

Russ called softly to the cat, who still remained in a fighting stance. Five minutes passed, and then ten. It seemed they would never get the cat out of the car.

Then suddenly, Russ began to sing. It was the same nonsensical song he'd sung to Bea on the mountain. He had a beautiful voice, mellow, soothing, almost bewitching. Ever so slowly, Miss Roosevelt was enchanted. She put one paw out and then the other, and finally she crept into his arm.

He emerged triumphantly from the car, cradling Miss Roosevelt in the blanket.

Then, with Bea watching over Macon and Ophie and the cat, Russ hooked the car to the winch on his truck and hauled it back onto the bridge.

It turned out that Macon and Ophie were on their way home, to Whitehaven, on the other side of Memphis. With Miss Ophie sitting on Macon's lap and Bea holding the still-pregnant cat, Russ delivered them home, towing their car. The Grimeses insisted on making hot chocolate and tuna sandwiches for everybody, and then Miss Roosevelt decided to have her kittens.

It was ten o'clock before Russ and Bea were on the road again.

They arrived in Florence in the wee hours of the morning. The Victorian house on North Wood Avenue was dark. Bea's mother and stepfather had long since given up waiting for her. She had called them from Memphis, letting them know what had gone wrong, telling them she hoped to be home sometime that evening.

In the graveled driveway, Russ turned off the engine. It chugged a while longer, then finally died. He patted the dashboard.

"This old baby made it, Bea. You're home safe."

"Thank you, Russ."

He hopped out and unloaded her bag. She got out on the other side and watched him. The Alabama night was bright with stars. One of the brightest seemed caught in his blond hair. When he glanced at her, his hair glowed like a halo.

My guardian angel, she thought.

"I guess this is really the end of the line, Bea."

Her throat got tight. She had to clear it before she could speak.

"I guess so."

He came around to her side of the truck.

"I'll carry your bag in, then I'll mosey on."

"Don't go."

She reached for him. They both looked down at their joined hands, then glanced away, embarrassed, uncertain and a little bit shy. She let him go.

"What I mean to say was—" pausing, she wet her lower lip with her tongue "—it's very late and you must be tired. You can stay here tonight."

"I don't want to impose."

"Impose! After all you've done for me? Don't be ridiculous."

"I'm never ridiculous."

They laughed together. Then they remembered how late it was, and they clamped their hands over their mouths.

"At times both of us are ridiculous, Russ." She lifted her hands, palms up, in appeal. "This house is full of empty bedrooms, and I owe you, anyway. Please come in and stay the night."

He considered her offer for a while. Every instinct told him to move on, but his heart cried *stay*. Knowing it was dangerous, knowing he shouldn't, he listened to his heart.

"Just the night." He retrieved his duffle bag and they went up the steps together. When they were standing in

front of the beveled glass door, a strange reluctance
overtook him. Here was a *real* home, a home where
people ate and slept and loved. He knew there was love
in this house. He felt it coming through the half-opened
doorway. He was both exhilarated and afraid.

"Bea, maybe this is not such a good idea. Your folks
don't know me, and I'm sure there are motels in this
town."

Her heart jumped up into her throat and sudden
panic seized her. She reached out and held on to his
arm.

"Don't go, Russ."

They stared at each other, full of yearnings and guilt.

*Why am I postponing this? It will only hurt more to-
morrow,* Russ thought.

Why can't I let him go? Bea wondered. *I'm being
selfish.*

Self-consciously, she took her hand off his arm and
stepped back from him.

"I won't keep you if you want to go, Russ."

"I'll stay."

She turned quickly from him so he wouldn't see her
smile of relief.

"Follow me, then."

They went inside and closed the door, being careful
not to make a racket.

"The bedrooms are upstairs," she whispered.

He followed her up the stairs. Like all old houses,
Bea's childhood home had its peculiar set of aches and
groans. The stairs creaked, the wooden floors popped,
and a few loose shutters flapped in the brisk night
breezes.

Bea led him to a high-ceilinged bedroom furnished
with heavy antiques and done in the colors of autumn.

It was the kind of room that could have been stiff and uninviting but wasn't. The room welcomed him, and he didn't quite know why. It could have been the light from the Victorian lamp Bea turned on. Or it might have been the Persian rug, faded but elegant. Or perhaps it was the row of family photographs, framed in silver, lined along the carved mantle.

"I think you'll find everything you need. The bathroom is over there." Bea waved her hand toward a closed door. "It's private. The sheets are clean, and the mattress is soft." She lingered in the doorway, strangely reluctant to leave. "Sleep well."

"Where will you be . . . in case I can't find everything I need."

"Right across the hall."

"I'll take your bag there."

"You've done enough already. I'm used to carrying my own bag."

"Not this time, Bea." He took her elbow and propelled her across the hall.

She opened the door to a room that was probably as cozy and inviting as his. He wouldn't know, for he couldn't see anything except the bed. A brass bed. Its covers were soft and satiny-looking, and soon it would hold Bea, soft and satiny herself, with her blacker-than-black hair spread on the pillow and her eyelashes touching her cool white cheeks.

His body went slack and he almost dropped the suitcase. Quickly he set it down.

"Good night, Russ."

Somehow "good night" didn't seem enough between them. He cupped her face between his palms. Bending down, he kissed her ever so gently. She opened her mouth, letting him taste the sweet honey inside. The bed gleamed at him, large and inviting. And he knew he had to let her go.

He stepped back and brushed a strand of dark hair off her cheek.

"Good night, Bea. Sleep well."

He left her then, left her standing in her bedroom with the brass bed, the soft sheets and the unspoken words. The door clicked shut behind him. He put his hand on her door, willing it to open again, willing her to be there for him, one more time. He waited for one heartbeat, two. Then he quickly crossed the hall, chastising himself.

"Russ Hammond, sometimes you are a selfish jerk."

He stripped off his jacket and shirt and tossed them on a chair. He would have taken Bea tonight. If she had said the word, he'd have entered her bedroom and carried her to that big brass bed and lost himself in the sweet mysteries of her body.

Her touch was healing, and he needed it. He needed her. But that's all it was, need. Not love, not commitment, merely need. She deserved more than that.

He finished undressing, then took a shower. The water was hot, the soap was fragrant, and the bath towel was fluffy. All the comforts of home, a real home.

He climbed into the antique bed and pulled the covers high over his chest. It had been an extraordinarily nerve-racking day, and he didn't expect to sleep. But sleep claimed him quickly.

He had been so tired, he had forgotten to turn off the light. A beam from the lamp fell across his beard as it rose and fell with the rhythm of his breathing.

Chapter Eight

The scream woke her up.

Bea sat straight up in her bed, clutching the sheet in her hands. The scream sounded again, and Bea came fully alert. She swung her feet over the side of her bed and raced out of her room.

Aunt Rachel was standing in the doorway of Russ's bedroom, screaming so hard the pink foam curlers in her hair were bouncing. Bea hurried across the hall and put her arm around Aunt Rachel's bony shoulders.

"Aunt Rachel, what on earth is the matter?"

Aunt Rachel turned around and squinted up at Bea. "Is that you, Bea?"

"It's me. Everything is all right."

"There's a naked man in my bed."

Aunt Rachel's finger shook as she pointed it toward the bed. Russ, disheveled and sleepy looking, was leaning against the headboard, trying to get the wadded sheet untangled enough to cover himself. He was showing all his chest, two very large feet and a good portion of impressive thigh.

He quite obviously was naked. Bea got sidetracked for a minute, then brought her mind back to the matter at hand.

"That's not your bed, Aunt Rachel."

"It most certainly is. When I got up this morning to brush my teeth, I left your Uncle Mack sleeping like a baby, and when I came back I found that naked man in my bed." Clutching Bea's sleeve, she ventured to lean into the room and shout, "What have you done with my Mack?"

"I can assure you, ma'am, that I'm harmless." Russ knotted the sheet around his waist and started to rise.

"Don't you move, you murderer. I wasn't born yesterday. I'm calling the cops."

The old woman started to leave, and Bea caught her by the shoulders.

"You're confused, Aunt Rachel. Russ Hammond is my guest."

"His picture is in every post office in this country. Most Wanted—that's the list he's on. I'd know that beard anywhere. What I want to know is, what's he doing in my bed?"

"You obviously took a wrong turn, Aunt Rachel. Let's go down the hall and see if we can't find Uncle Mack."

"I'm never wrong, Bea. I've never been wrong in all my eighty-six years. Mack can vouch for that."

Bea felt helpless in the face of such logic. She glanced at Russ to see how he was taking it all. He was leaning against the headboard, laughing.

"What's going on up here?" Glory Ethel Adams Rakestraw appeared at the head of the stairs and came down the hallway, wearing her pink flannel robe and her fuzzy rabbit slippers. When she saw Bea, she opened her arms and broke into a huge grin. "Darling, Bea." She hugged her daughter close. "When did you get in?"

"Late last night, Mother. We didn't want to wake anybody."

"I'm so glad you're here. Jedidiah and I were beginning to worry about you."

"Glory Ethel," Aunt Rachel interrupted. "There's a naked man in my bed."

Glory Ethel glanced into the room. "Hello, I'm Bea's mother. You must be the nice young man who brought Bea home."

"Russ Hammond, Mrs. Rakestraw."

"Welcome to our home." Glory Ethel took Aunt Rachel firmly by the arm. "Rachel, there hasn't been a naked man in your bed for years. Let's go down the hall and find Mack." She winked at Bea over her shoulder. "Carry on, Bea."

"She's a terrific lady," Russ said.

"She's the best."

Russ reclined on the bed, drinking in the sight of Bea in her white satin gown. Her shoulders were bare, and her hips were outlined by the fit and flare of the silky skirt. Until he saw her he hadn't realized how much he loved the intimacy of being with a woman in feminine lingerie.

"I'm sorry Aunt Rachel woke you, Russ. I'll close your door so you can go back to sleep." Bea put her hand on the door.

"Don't go."

"You must be exhausted. I know I am."

"You're right, I'm tired." Russ reknotted the sheet quickly then got out of bed, wearing the sheet with the flare of a magnificent Roman gladiator. "But more than that, I'm starved—" he started slowly across the room toward her "—starved for the sight of a lovely woman in a white satin gown."

He was even with her now. She trembled inside, but she tried not to let it show. Taking her arm, he pulled her inside and closed the door.

"Russ..."

"I just want to look, Bea."

He cupped her face, his touch as careful as if he were handling rare porcelain.

"White satin does beautiful things to a woman's skin, Bea." His thumbs caressed her chin. "Your skin looks delicious."

"This is dangerous, Russ."

"I know." He moved his hands down to her shoulders. "Are you afraid?"

"No."

"I didn't think so." He let his fingertips drift slowly across her upper chest, tracing the neckline of her gown. He left a small trail of goose bumps.

"That's more than looking, Russ."

"I'm selfish. I want to touch, too."

She closed her eyes and let her head fall back. He leaned down and kissed the pulse point at the base of her throat.

"Please," she whispered.

"I know." His mouth slid up the side of her throat.

"We are so wrong for each other."

"Always have been." He skimmed her lips, sipping lightly of her sweetness.

"Russ." Her voice was muffled underneath his.

"Only one kiss...Bea...one kiss to wake up to." His arms encircled her and he molded her body against his.

With exquisite tenderness, he kissed her good morning. Everything that was good and right and beautiful poured forth in the kiss.

And when it was over, he released her.

"Thank you, Bea. You're a kind and generous woman."

She touched his cheek, ever so softly. Then dragging her fingers down his fine cheekbones, she tangled them in the crisp curls of his beard.

"You are a dangerous man, Russ, an irresistible pirate."

"It's too bad we're not suited to each other."

"Too bad." She opened the door and started to leave. Halfway into the hall, she turned back to him. "Russ, if I asked you to stay a few more days, would you?"

"Why do you want me to stay, Bea?"

"I don't know."

"Don't you?"

They watched each other as intently as if the fate of the world hinged on seeing each blink of the eye, each twitch of muscle, each ragged breath. Unconsciously Russ leaned toward her, drawn by some irresistible force he didn't dare name.

Bea took one step back into the room and then another and another, and finally she was running, running to the haven of his arms. He embraced her, fitting her head against his shoulder. Her breath was hot on his skin and her voice was muffled when she spoke.

"All I can think of is you sitting on that bridge singing to a pregnant cat." She pressed closer to him, whispering, "Dear Lord in heaven, I'm afraid to understand why I want you here."

He was afraid, too, but he didn't show his fear. Instead, he tenderly stroked her—her hair, her arms, her back.

"Don't be afraid, Bea. I'm here."

"Russ..."

"Shh. I'm here. I'll stay."

They held on to each other until the exquisite tenderness of their embrace turned to awareness, until the awareness bordered on passion. And then he let her go. Contenting himself with one kiss, pressed hard against her soft cheek, he let her go.

She turned quickly before he could see the tears in her eyes. Her bare feet made no sound as she moved toward the door. She wanted to look back, she wanted to run to him, she wanted to climb into his arms and into his bed and never leave. Never. But she knew that was a foolish and impossible dream.

By the time she had reached her room, tears stung her cheeks in earnest. When she was safely inside, she leaned against her door. Every thought of sleep was driven from her mind. All she could think about was the way she felt when Russ Hammond touched her.

She put two fingers on her lips and pressed.

"What kind of fool are you, Bea Adams?"

The old grandfather clock in the downstairs hall bonged the hour—six o'clock. Bea straightened her shoulders and marched to her closet. She was home now and everything would be all right. Even when Russ left, everything would be all right. She'd keep telling herself that until she believed it.

Russ was glad he'd decided to stay.

By ten o'clock, the house on North Wood Avenue

was filled with people, lively people who laughed a lot and hugged a lot and talked a lot. He felt rejuvenated.

"I thought you might need this." A big handsome man thrust a glass of iced tea into Russ's hands. Samuel Adams, Bea's brother. "Talking to this crew can make a man thirsty."

"Thanks." Russ took the cool glass.

"I really appreciate what you did for my sister."

"I was glad to lend a hand."

"It seems you did more than lend a hand. You did an all-out rescue job." Samuel laughed. "And with my sister, that's not easy."

"She *is* independent."

"*Bossy* is the word I'd have used."

"That, too."

Russ felt himself being inspected. He didn't mind. If he'd had a sister like Bea, he'd have done the same thing.

"Do I measure up?"

Samuel's dark eyes crinkled at the corners when he laughed. "You caught me redhanded."

"I don't blame you. I'm sure that nothing you've seen about me inspires confidence."

"I never judge a man by appearances."

"Then you are a rarity. A wise man."

"You might not have said that two years ago."

Russ saw Samuel glance across the room at a gorgeous blond woman, big in her pregnancy. She was a paradox, a woman who appeared to be both angel and devilish prankster. And from the expression on Samuel's face, it was obvious that he adored the woman. She was Molly, if Russ remembered correctly, Samuel's wife.

"Two years ago when I first met Molly, I made the mistake of judging by appearances. My wife taught me a lesson I'll never forget." Samuel threw back his head and laughed with uninhibited joy as he remembered his courtship.

He was still laughing when Bea joined them. She hooked her hand through Russ's arm. That alone was unusual. Bea had never so clearly and blatantly identified herself with one man. What Samuel saw next was even more startling. Bea looked directly into Russ's eyes and smiled. Samuel saw trust in the smile, and friendship and joy. But most of all, he saw love. Having learned love the hard way, he was quick to recognize it.

Two years ago, before Molly, Samuel would have run a thorough check on Russ Hammond. He'd have found out about his background, his business, his financial security, his habits, his friends. Now he merely relaxed and trusted that his sister had enough sense to know what she was doing. And if she made a mistake—which wasn't likely—he'd be there to help her.

"You have flour on your nose, Bea." Samuel leaned over and wiped the tip of his sister's nose. "Does that mean you've been cooking?"

Bea's color heightened. "Aunt Rachel insisted on giving me a private lesson. 'Beatrice,' she said, 'no Southern woman would be caught dead making sawmill gravy with lumps.' Naturally, I agreed."

Samuel and Russ hooted with laughter.

"In order to keep the peace." Bea grinned at them. "Russ found out the hard way that it doesn't do to get Aunt Rachel's dander up."

"That story has already made the rounds," Samuel said. "I understand there is even a movement among the unmarried cousins to have a repeat performance."

"I think I'll decline. I don't like to be center stage more than once a visit."

"Aunt Rachel is terribly sorry about what happened, Russ," Bea told him. "She wants to make it up to you."

"There was no harm done. In fact, I rather enjoyed it. I haven't had that much attention since I turned a frog loose in the fourth-grade classroom."

"Humor her. She doesn't want to apologize. She just wants you to come into the kitchen and lick the bowl."

"Lick the bowl?"

"Don't look a gift horse in the mouth," Samuel told him. "Licking the bowl is a rare privilege, especially if Aunt Rachel is making her famous divinity."

"Her divinity?"

"Candy," Bea explained, laughing. "Why don't you just come with me and find out."

Aunt Rachel was bustling around the kitchen, wearing two aprons, one a frilly organdy and the other a cotton domestic to protect her *company* apron. A perky red bow—the kind used on Christmas packages—perched in her sparse gray hair. In order to keep her bow from toppling off into the gravy, she had stretched a hairnet over her head, anchoring it with enough bobby pins to keep a drugstore in business for a year of two.

She waved when Russ and Bea entered the kitchen.

"Well . . . I said to Bea, I said, why don't you get that nice young man out here and let me show him a thing or two? Didn't I say that, Bea?" She never stopped talking long enough for Bea to reply, but kept looking up at Russ, craning her neck up so that she could see beyond the full beard that so fascinated her. "I said, I'll bet that young man would like to lick the bowl. I never saw a man yet who didn't. 'The way to a man's heart,'

and all that, that's what I've always said. You just ask
Mack. Mack can tell you. 'The way to a man's heart,'
just you wait and see. Mack will tell you. It works
everytime.''

Bea winked at Russ over the top of Aunt Rachel's
head. He smiled down at the two women. It had been a
long, long time since he'd been in a real kitchen. This
one was big and cozy with copper pots hanging from the
ceiling and coffee perking on the stove and bread bak-
ing in the oven and pots of daisies sitting in the sunshine on the windowsill.

He was enchanted.

"Bea tells me you're making divinity, Aunt Rachel."

"That's just like her, telling all my secrets." Aunt
Rachel plucked a big white apron off a hook. "Bend
over," she told Russ, "I'm going to introduce you to the
joys of cooking."

"I confess that I'm rather ignorant in that field."

"You don't need a degree to beat divinity. Just a good
strong arm and lots of patience. That's what I always
tell Mack, lots of patience, I say." She looped the sashes
around Russ, then tied them in a tiny knot. "My, you're
a big man. There's not enough sash to make a bow on
you.''

"Bea—" Aunt Rachel turned to her niece who sat on
a stool in a patch of sunshine, watching "—I'm so glad
you picked out a big man this time. You never used to
date anybody except those scrawny bookish types. I'll
bet they couldn't even hold out to beat the divinity."

"I'll bet they couldn't, either." Russ gave Bea a
wicked smile and followed Aunt Rachel to the kitchen
counter.

He was having a wonderful time. Bea could tell by his
jaunty walk and the easy way he smiled and joked with

Aunt Rachel. Not for all the tea in China would she have spoiled his fun by arguing about the men she had dated. Come to think of it, they *had* been rather anemic looking. She'd bet they couldn't hold out to beat the divinity, either.

Russ and Aunt Rachel had their heads together, earnestly discussing the process of stirring the candy until it was exactly the right consistency.

"Can I do anything to help, Aunt Rachel?" Bea asked.

"You just sit still over there and watch two pros at work."

Bea did as she was told. One of the things she loved about coming back every year to her family's reunion was the everydayness of things. Life in this big old house in Florence was filled with reassuring routines and ordinary pleasures—setting the coffee on to perk first thing in the morning, raising the shades to let the sunshine in, flicking off the night-light in the bathroom, running over to a neighbor's house for a cup of tea. As she sat on her kitchen stool, a sense of peace stole over her. Life from this angle looked good, and it suddenly seemed full of possibilities.

She propped her hand on her chin and lost herself in observing Russ. He looked *right* in the kitchen, with a white apron straining over his broad chest and a big metal spoon in his hand. He was laughing, and it was a sound of such uninhibited delight that Bea wanted to capture it in a bottle and keep it forever. She could imagine herself uncapping that bottle when she felt blue, listening once more to the sound of his laughter and feeling uplifted.

"You can lick the bowl now," Aunt Rachel's voice interrupted Bea's thoughts.

Russ dipped his finger into the bowl and came up with a glob of white sugary candy. He poked it into his mouth and grinned.

"Hmm, no wonder it's called divinity." He ran his finger around the edge of the bowl and came up with another generous dollop. "Here, Bea. Try this."

He stood in front of her, offering his finger. She bent over and slowly took his finger into her mouth. It was heaven. Not the candy, but the taste of the man. His finger pads were slightly calloused and felt rough against her tongue. There were crisp little hairs along the tops of his fingers that tickled the inside of her mouth. His skin had an overall salty taste that set all her nerve endings atingle.

"There's more in the bowl," Aunt Rachel said.

Bea suddenly realized she was still holding on to Russ's finger. To make matters worse, he was staring down at her as if he'd invented her and planned to gloat over his invention until sometime next Tuesday.

She opened her mouth slowly, like a baby bird, and he withdrew his finger.

"Wasn't that good?" he asked.

She didn't think he was talking about the candy.

"Wonderful."

She wasn't talking about candy, either.

They stared at each other, their eyes wide and aware, until Aunt Rachel plucked Russ's sleeve, pulling him back across the kitchen to another cooking project of hers.

Bea decided she'd better rescue him or else Aunt Rachel would keep him there the rest of the morning. The funny thing was, he didn't look as if he wanted rescuing. He was having the time of his life.

The kitchen door banged open and five of the row-diest children in the clan catapulted into the kitchen, making the question of rescue moot. Eight-year-old Sim was tossing a football into the air, and two-year-old Ralph was tagging along behind, sucking his thumb and dragging his blanket and saying, "Me wanna p'ay, me wanna p'ay."

"Goodness gracious, children," Aunt Rachel said, ducking out of the way of the ball. "Take that ball outside."

Sim, the leader, puffed out his chest and craned his neck up at Russ.

"Them's neat boots, mister."

"Thanks," Russ said.

"You sure are big."

"I guess I am."

"I'll betcha played ball."

"As a matter of fact, I did." Russ bent over the small boys, gathering three of them in his arms. "Why don't you fellows take me outside and we'll have a game or two?"

"Aw *right!*" Sim turned proudly to his cousins. "See, I told you he was a nice dude." Then he marched toward the door, his cowlick flopping as he led the pack outside.

When Russ passed Bea's stool, he picked her up, then set her on her feet. "How about it, Tiger Lady? Want to play with me?"

Dear lord in heaven, did she want to play with him? Yes, yes, yes.

"No," she said, to be on the safe side. "I suppose I'd better stay and help Aunt Rachel."

"Shoo. Scoot. Scat." Aunt Rachel swished her apron at them. "Get on out of the kitchen and let me finish up in here. Go on now, before I have to take a broom and sweep you out.''

Russ's smile was as gleeful as a child's.

''Looks like you're stuck with me, Tiger Lady.'' He draped his arm around her shoulders as if it belonged there and led her out into the backyard.

Little children romped in the sunshine, their laughter high and spiraling, their sturdy legs pumping up and down as they tried to catch a bird and put salt on his tail. Russ felt the tug of home on his heartstrings. With Bea tucked safely under his arm and the laughter of children ringing in his ears and the smell of home cooking wafting through the screen door, he longed for home. Not just any home, but *his* home. A home he could call his own, a home with children and laughter and a wife who welcomed him with a kiss, a home with a dog curled in front of the fireplace and lots of books scattered on the bookshelves and tables, a home with a front porch and rocking chairs so he could sit outside in June and watch the fireflies.

It suddenly occurred to him that perhaps he'd been running scared for too long. Perhaps some things were worth taking risks for.

''Catch, mister.'' Sim tossed the ball Russ's way, and Russ became tangled in a group of squirming, screaming children.

Bea sat on a swing under a magnolia tree, marveling at his ease with children, until he swooped by and tugged her into the game. She hadn't romped that way since she was a child. In Dallas she'd never have considered tumbling on the ground and getting grass in her hair, but in Florence, with Russ at her side, it seemed the most natural thing in the world. And besides that, it was fun.

They were both breathless when the children finally tired of the game and moved on to bigger and better things—trying to dig a crawdad hole to China.

Russ and Bea sat side by side in the swing. It moved gently in the autumn morning, propelled by Russ, who occasionally pushed them off with one foot.

"I'm glad I stayed, Bea."

"So am I."

He reached out and covered her hand with his. "A man could get addicted to all this."

"So could a woman."

"How did you end up in Dallas, Bea?"

"Like most small-town girls, I longed for bright lights and big cities. I suppose I thought life would be better there, happier, fuller, richer." She paused, looking out across the yard. "Funny how we don't really appreciate the things we have until we're far away from them."

"Have you ever thought of coming back?"

She swiveled her head to look at him.

"Coming back?"

"Here. To Florence."

"From time to time, I suppose. But my mother is happily married now, and so is Samuel. There doesn't seem to be much point in coming back."

They sat on the swing, holding hands and thinking of life and its many winding roads, and both of them wondered at their choices. Had they taken the right roads? Or had they turned left when they should have gone straight?

Russ was full of longings and needs that he couldn't quite comprehend. And Bea was wishing for things she thought she couldn't have.

And so the minutes passed by, and soon it was time to go inside for lunch.

* * *

Glory Ethel gathered the clan together in what she called her ballroom. Flushed and smiling, she rang a small silver bell. The noise in the room gradually died down.

"Every year," she said, "the Adams clan gathers in Florence to celebrate the unity of family. And every year it seems our family grows. Two years ago my husband, Jedidiah Rakestraw, joined us for the first time. Jedidiah." Smiling, she held her hand toward her husband. He came forward and linked his arm through hers. At seventy-five he was still as erect and lively as a man fifteen years younger.

"A few months later," she continued, "Jedidiah's beautiful daughter Molly won the heart of Florence's die-hard bachelor—my son, Samuel Adams." There was a general hubbub of comments and laughter. "And soon, Jedidiah and I will be grandparents for the first time." She smiled at Samuel and Molly. "The Adams family continues to grow. Rachel and Mack's granddaughter has her fiancé with her this year, and Howard and Lucille are going to be grandparents for the fifth time."

"Sixth," Howard Adams corrected his sister-in-law.

"I must be getting old." Glory Ethel laughed.

"Never." Jedidiah leaned over and kissed his wife's cheek. "You'll never grow old, Glory Ethel."

"On that fine note, let's eat.... No. Wait." Glory Ethel held up her hand. "My daughter's friend, Russ Hammond, is with us this year. We welcome him."

"Daddy," a child in the back of the room said, "can't we ever eat?"

With much laughter and good-natured teasing, the Adams clan began their meal. Glory Ethel loved parties and had outdone herself for this one. Folding tables had been set up, and each one sported a lace-edged white cloth and a bouquet of fall flowers. The long buffet table along the south wall was fairly groaning with food—ham and biscuits and fried chicken and sawmill gravy and beans, snapped fresh from Aunt Sukie's garden and kept frozen till the reunion; cakes and cookies and tarts and pies, made from the apples straight from Uncle Howard's backyard tree.

Bea and Russ sat at the table with Samuel and Molly. The meal was lively with lots of laughter and plenty of good conversation. Russ had almost forgotten what it was like to be in a crowd. And he couldn't remember what it was like to be part of a family. He had no living relatives, and neither had Lurlene. So even their brief marriage had not provided him with a sense of belonging to some larger clan, of being a part of a family.

Had he been wrong all those years? In being afraid to love, had he deprived himself of something precious?

Before he could continue pondering the choices he'd made and their consequences, Molly leaned toward him to tell a funny story about Glory Ethel and Jedidiah in Paris.

Suddenly all the conversation in the room stopped. Two women at the table behind Russ gasped, and Bea's face turned white. He reached for her hand.

"Bea. What's the matter?"

She didn't answer. Her eyes were fixed on the doorway. Russ turned and saw a man standing there, a tall handsome man who bore a striking resemblance to both Bea and Samuel Adams.

"At ease, folks. I'm not a ghost." The man's dark eyes darted around the gathering, taking in everything. When he found Bea and Samuel, he strode forward.

"It's Taylor Adams. Mack, it's your nephew, Taylor." Aunt Rachel's voice carried around the room. "He has his gall."

Bea watched in astonishment as her father came toward her table. He'd said he was not a ghost, but he might as well have been. In her heart, he'd been dead since he'd walked out on her mother more than twenty years ago.

She gripped the edge of the table, hoping she was in the middle of a nightmare, hoping she'd wake up and discover she'd been dreaming. But he was real; she heard his voice, saw his black eyes. And he kept on coming.

When he was at their table, Taylor Adams stopped. Leaning down, he kissed Molly's cheek. "My dear, you look lovely." Then he reached out and gripped his son's hand. "Samuel. Good to see you."

Bea was frozen, speechless. Her brother was sitting across the table acting as if he'd seen Taylor yesterday, acting as if the man had done nothing more than leave them for a Sunday stroll.

"Bea." Taylor's voice was deep and rich as it had always been. She used to love for him to read bedtime stories to her. "You're more beautiful than I could ever imagine."

He came around the table toward her. She suddenly found the strength to move. Without saying a word, she left the table.

"Bea." It was Taylor, calling after her.

She kept on going. *Let him call. Let him see what it felt like to be left behind.* She maintained her dignity all the way to the door. Once she was out of sight of the relatives, she bolted. There was only one place she could go. She made her way down the hall and through the kitchen, intensely aware of the smell of fried chicken. The smell made her sick. She would never eat chicken again.

The back door shut behind her. She began to run, run so fast that she lost one of her shoes. She kept on going. The thick grove of trees loomed ahead of her. She began to stumble, unaware that tears blinded her.

"Dammit, dammit, dammit. Why did you have to come back?"

She entered the grove and sank to her knees. Pine needles and fallen leaves made a thick brown cushion. A squirrel, angry at her intrusion, chattered at her then scurried up a water oak tree and sat scolding on a branch.

She was sick to her stomach. Leaning over, she heaved, but nothing came up. She bowed her head and clutched at the earth.

"Bea."

She didn't even look up.

"Go away, Samuel."

"No, Bea." He sat down beside her.

She turned accusing eyes toward him. "You knew, didn't you? You knew he'd be coming."

"Yes."

"How? Why?"

"How is a long story. After I married Molly, I realized that I couldn't keep hiding my head in the sand. Taylor Adams left us. That's true. But he's still our father."

"Maybe he's yours. He's not mine."

"Yes, he is, Bea. What he did doesn't change that."

"A father takes care of his children. He picks them up and carries them to bed every night. He reads them stories and teaches them to play ball and cheers at their

school plays and cries at their graduation. Taylor didn't
do any of that."

"That wasn't entirely his fault, Bea."

"Are you saying it was Mother's fault? How dare
you!"

"Bea, I'm not saying Taylor didn't make a terrible
mistake. I'm not saying he was a good father. He wasn't
there to talk to us or to bandage our wounds or to cheer
us on. But he *did* make some provisions for us."

"What provisions?"

"Through Uncle Howard. I only found out about it
two years ago." Samuel smoothed his sister's hair as he
talked. He knew the healing power of touch. Molly had
taught him that. "He set aside trust funds for our edu-
cation. Mother was too proud to use them. She was determined to make it on her own."

"She did, too. She didn't need Taylor Adams. *I* don't
need Taylor Adams."

"You do. You need him and you just don't know it."

"What can he do for me now? Watch while I go to
my fancy office? Take credit when I draw my big sal-
ary?" Fury made her eyes black. "What I am is due to
my own ability and the love of my mother and my
brother. I don't owe him a damned thing, not even a
decent hello."

"You owe yourself, Bea."

"It's not like you to pussyfoot around, Samuel. Tell
it to me straight. I'm a big girl. I can take it."

"Then I'll tell you straight out. We invited Taylor
here."

"*You.*"

"Yes. Mother knew. We had her blessing."

"Why didn't you tell me?"

"Would you have come?"

Bea was thoughtful for a moment, then she answered with typical honesty. "No."

"That's what I thought. That's why I didn't tell you."

"What do you want me to do, Samuel? Go in there and hug him and kiss his cheek like a good little girl? Go in there and pretend he's my daddy?"

"Dammit." Bea rarely saw her brother explode, but he did now. "You're just as all-fired stubborn now as you were when you were ten years old."

"Maybe I am, Samuel. I don't know." She picked at the grass and pine needles. "Go away. Go back inside to Molly. I want to be alone."

Samuel had always been sensitive to her moods, and now he stood up to leave. Bea knew he didn't want to. Samuel was a fixer. He hated to leave something behind that he couldn't fix.

To soften the blow, she reached for his hand and smiled up at him.

"Tell Aunt Rachel to save me a piece of pie."

When Samuel got back to the house, Russ was waiting for him in the hallway.

"How is she? What did she say? What is she doing?"

Samuel reached for his pipe, and then remembered that he hadn't smoked in years.

"She's out back in the grove, just as I knew she would be. And she's fine. She just wants to be alone."

As Samuel talked, he studied the play of emotions on Russ Hammond's face.

"I know you wanted to go after her, Russ. I want to thank you for letting me do it. There were some things I had to tell her."

"And did you?"

"Yes." Samuel recognized that protective tone in Russ's voice. It was one he used himself with Molly, beautiful, sweet, playful Molly. Contentment rose in him like yeast until he was swollen with it, bursting with pride and joy and deep, abiding satisfaction.

Russ stood beside him, watchful, barely restraining his urge to ask questions, to demand answers. Samuel saw all of that, and he understood. Suddenly he came to a decision.

"Come into the library with me, Russ. There are some things I want you to know. Family things."

When they were seated in leather chairs and locked behind closed doors, Samuel told Russ Hammond the story of Taylor Adams. Russ listened without comment.

He sat silently long after the sound of Samuel's voice had died away, and then he stood up.

"Thank you, Samuel." He took Samuel's hand in a firm grip, and then turned toward the door.

"Where are you going?"

"To Bea. The last thing she needs right now is to be alone."

Chapter Nine

"Samuel said I'd find you here."

Bea squeezed the pine needles in her hand and glanced over her shoulder. Russ was three feet from her, looking as solid and tranquil as the tree beside him, holding on to the shoe she'd lost in the yard.

"I told Samuel I wanted to be alone."

"He relayed that message." Russ sat down beside her, tossed the shoe aside and pulled her into his arms. "You're hurting, Bea. Lean on me."

She fought the urge to bury her face against his chest and cry. "I don't need to lean. I need to be strong." She sat stiffly in the curve of his arms, determined to be strong.

"You need me, Bea. And I'm not going to let you go."

"I don't need anybody. Not you, and certainly not Taylor Adams."

"Don't fight it, Bea. Don't keep running away."

"I'm not running away. I'm sitting in the sunshine watching the squirrels."

She turned her face away so he wouldn't see the truth in her eyes. She needed him, needed him more than she'd ever needed anything or anyone in her life. And it scared her to death. In spite of her resolutions to be strong and mature and intelligent, she was still scared.

But not as scared as she had been before Russ sat down beside her, not as scared as she had been until he put his arm around her shoulder. She wanted to cuddle up to him the way she had on the mountain during the thunderstorm, but she knew she shouldn't. He'd be leaving soon. He'd go back to traveling the roads in his pickup truck, and she'd have to get used to doing without him.

The thought made her feel hollow inside.

"Bea." Russ cupped her chin with one hand and gently turned her face toward his. "I'm here if you want to talk."

"Talk about what?"

"Your father." He held her chin and studied her face. What he saw made him sad; he saw hurt in her eyes and rejection.

If he ever needed wisdom, he needed it now. Gazing down at Bea, he felt the urge to be everything for her— her confidante, her counselor, her friend, her protector. But most of all, he felt the need to ease her loneliness. And the only way he knew to do that was to touch—and to share.

"I barely remember my father." Turning his face away from hers, he spoke softly, as if he were trying hard not to wake too many memories. "I was so young when he died.... Over the years I suppose I've created him, made him larger than life."

He rubbed her upper arms as he talked, gently, up and down, up and down. *I'm here,* his touch was saying. *I'm here for you, Bea.*

"I don't know what he would have been like if he had lived. Maybe he would have been a careless father or a negligent father or even an absentee father."

"Like Taylor," she said.

"Like Taylor," Russ agreed. "But a father, still."

Bea pressed closer to him. She felt comforted. Safe.

"I never knew you didn't have a father."

"Nor a mother. I grew up with a series of foster parents."

"At least you had two parents to love you."

"They were paid to keep me, Bea. Not to love me."

"Russ," she said softly, turning and putting her hand on his cheek. How could anyone not have loved Russ? She felt broken inside. And selfish. And guilty. "I'm so sorry, Russ. So sorry."

He turned her hand over and kissed her palm. Then, because it felt right, he kissed it again, lingering until he had absorbed the fragrance and texture of her skin.

"I guess what I'm saying, Bea, is that we don't often get second chances to have a father, a *real* father."

She watched the squirrels playing in the trees. Then she turned her attention to a mockingbird, scolding and chattering nearby. How easy it would be to drift along, letting nature take its course. Taylor would leave; he couldn't stay forever. And she could wait him out, just sit back and watch from a distance until he gave up and went away.

"I remember growing up in this house, Russ." She propped her elbow on her knees and cupped her chin. "I remember running home from school sometimes, hoping that Taylor had come back, wishing he would be in the kitchen waiting for me, holding a glass of milk and some cookies and telling some silly story about why he had gone away. I imagined he'd say he had gone to be a circus clown so he could learn to make his children laugh, or that he had gone out west so he could come back and tell us authentic cowboy stories."

"Children often wish for things they can't have, Bea. I wished for a pet—a puppy, a turtle, a goldfish. I didn't care, as long as I had something to call my own."

"Did you get a pet, Russ?"

"Once. I had an old stray dog two weeks before he died." He put his hand on the back of her neck and laced his fingers through her dark hair. "Bea, we're not children anymore."

"Are you telling me to grow up?" She turned and smiled at him.

"No. I'm telling you that you have a choice to make. You didn't have a father when you were a child, but it seems that you can have one now."

"What would you do, Russ?"

He sat very still, his eyes darkening as he studied her. Overhead a mockingbird scolded a squirrel, and it scampered away, sending a shower of autumn leaves drifting downward. Two gold leaves caught in Bea's dark hair.

Russ's stomach tightened. He remembered another time, another place, another woman with blossoms in her hair. Need ripped through him, but it wasn't Lurlene he wanted. It wasn't Lurlene who made his pulse quicken and his breathing ragged: it was a woman with dark eyes and gold leaves tangled in her black hair.

"If I were you," he said, "I would kiss me."

"You would?" Her eyes widened and her face grew soft. "Why?"

"Because it would taste good."

Bea's pulse quickened, and she felt a lethargy creeping over her.

"Anything else?" she asked, her voice hardly more than a whisper.

"Because it would feel good."

She tipped her face up to his. Not unconsciously, but deliberately. She was making a choice, a choice to give something back to this wonderful man who had given her so much.

"And..." she whispered.

His hands bracketed her face and he bent over her, so close she could feel his beard tickle her chin.

"And—" his head dipped lower "—because I need you and you need me."

As if fate had decreed it, he lowered his mouth to hers. She welcomed him, weaving her arms around his neck and pulling him so close he could feel her heart beating against his.

"Ahh, Bea." He tipped her head back and trailed his open mouth down the side of her throat. The fragrance of spring flowers made him dizzy. "You take away my lonesomeness...."

He pressed his mouth over the pulse beating softly at the base of her throat. She had never known a man's lips could feel like home. She felt passion, certainly. And desire. Such desire as she had never known.

But most of all, she felt as if she had come home.

"Russ...Russ..." She said his name over and over, loving the way it sounded, the way it felt on her tongue.

He lowered her to a carpet of pine needles and stretched full length on top of her, being careful not to crush her under his weight.

"A public place," he said, "but I can't resist."

"The bower is secluded. No one will see."

He pulled her hard against his chest, and they rolled together, mouths locked and legs entwined. The passion that had been simmering between them since that night in the Quachita Mountains exploded. She pulled his shirt loose from his waistband and slid her hands over his bare back. He moaned and pressed his hips against hers. Through the layers of clothes, through his jeans and her wool slacks, she could feel the heat and the size of him.

"Ahhh, Russ . . ."

"Yes . . . Bea . . . yes." His tongue delved into her mouth, and her nails raked his back.

"You feel so good, Bea. You taste so good." He murmured to her softly between kisses. "You almost make me believe in love."

His words drifted slowly through the fog of desire that clouded her brain and finally sank in. Her hands stilled. What was she doing? She was dangerously close to giving her heart to a man who didn't believe in love, a man who freely admitted that he would have left his wife if she hadn't left him first. Russ Hammond was wonderful and kind and understanding and chivalrous and lovely to look at, but he was a drifter, a man who would hit the road when the notion struck.

She didn't think she could stand any more goodbyes of the important kind, goodbyes to people she loved. It was best all around not to fall in love.

"Russ?"

"Hmm?"

She shivered as he nibbled the tender skin below her ear. "I want to thank you for all you've done."

"To thank me?" He lifted himself on his elbow and gazed down at her.

"Yes." She caught her lower lip between her teeth, then turned her face away from his. She couldn't look at him. If she did, she might change her mind. And then, heaven help them all. "And to pay you, Russ. I've never paid you."

"You want to give me money, Bea?"

"Yes. That was our bargain."

Russ sat up, taking Bea with him. He kept one arm draped around her shoulder because he couldn't bear to let her go, not yet. Then he gazed upward into the pines. A ray of sunlight filtered down through the thick branches.

It seemed to him that he was always seeing sunlight from a distance, that it never quite reached him, never quite touched him with its warmth. Turning, he looked at the white Victorian house. Such a homey, comfortable house. A man could get used to living in a house like that. Or any house, for that matter.

No, he corrected himself. Not any house. A special house. One with clean sheets and polished floors and a hall clock that ticked and a beautiful woman who waited at the windows, watching for the man she loved to come home.

It was foolish of him to be dreaming. Bea was out of his reach, always had been, always would be. And anyhow, he hadn't given himself permission to be reaching, not on any permanent basis, anyhow. He guessed fatigue had made him see things in a crooked, upside-down way.

He turned back to Bea, his smile tinged with sadness. Bea Adams didn't need him anymore.

Whatever happened, she could handle it without him. Oh, maybe not as well as if he were there. But, hell, he couldn't hang around indefinitely, waiting for her car to quit or for kidnappers to come or for somebody to get stuck on a bridge. It was time for both of them to get on with their lives.

"Bea." He turned and cupped her face, holding it almost fiercely. "You've been one of the best times of my life."

"That sounds like goodbye."

"It is. You don't need me anymore, Bea."

"But, Russ..."

She needed him so much, the need was almost a physical pain. But she didn't tell him that. So...they had felt passion for each other. That was nothing unusual between a man and a woman, especially two people who had been forced into such close company. If her passion bordered on love, that was her problem, not his.

She squared her shoulders and smiled at him.

"You've been a good knight in shining armor."

His fingers tenderly traced her cheekbones. "If I ever run across another damsel in distress, I hope she's half as delightful as you." His hand lingered on her cheek. "Goodbye, Tiger Lady."

She had to clear the lump in her throat before she could speak.

"You could stay for the rest of the family reunion."

"I'll go."

"Everybody in the family loves...likes you, Russ. We'd all be happy for you to stay longer."

"I might get addicted to families."

Suddenly she felt something close to panic. What would she do without Russ? Not that she needed him to take care of her. No. That wasn't it at all. Somehow, somewhere, sometime he had become a part of her, and his going would divide her so that the joy and laughter vanished and the lonesome part stayed behind.

She knew that was crazy. She kept telling herself that it was crazy. She pressed her hand over her mouth to swallow words she had no business saying.

"Bea." Russ's hands moved over her face, ceaselessly, committing her to memory. "Thank you for the invitation, Bea." He kissed her mouth swiftly, so he wasn't tempted to stay.

Then he stood up to leave. Bea felt too weak to stand. She tipped her head back so she could see his face. The sun slanted through the trees, tipping his hair and his beard with gold. She would always remember him that way.

"Good luck, Russ." She wouldn't speak of money again. Instinctively she knew he wouldn't take it. To speak of payment now, after all that had happened between them, would be insulting. "Take care. *Do* take care."

"Thank you, Tiger Lady."

He was leaving the bower when he remembered the shoe he'd found in the dirt. It was lying on its side among the pine needles. He scooped it up.

"I believe Cinderella has lost her shoe." He held it aloft.

"But not at the ball."

"And this is not a Prince Charming who found it."

"There have been times over the last few days when I could argue that point." Her smile was tempered with the sadness of saying goodbye.

"If I were Prince Charming and you were Cinderella..." He paused, reaching for her. She extended her leg and he caught it midcalf. His fingers kneaded her tense muscles through her slacks; then he slid his hand slowly down to her foot. With great tenderness he slipped the shoe on. Still holding her foot, he looked at her, gazing so deeply into her eyes he seemed to be seeing her soul. "The shoe fits. If the fairy tale were true, I'd have to make you my princess."

She couldn't tear her gaze away. There was magic in his blue eyes, and humor and passion and promises she couldn't read. Her breath escaped in a small sigh.

"We should both be grateful it was just a fairy tale." Her tongue flicked out and wet her lower lip. "Two people like us... so different."

"So very different." He reached up and cupped her face. "Goodbye, Bea Adams."

"Russ..."

He didn't give her time to finish, but rose quickly and left the grove, never looking back. It wouldn't do to look back. If he looked back, if he saw her sitting there with gold leaves falling in her hair, he might never go. He might pick her up and carry her to his truck and ride away with her, south toward Florida, south where the breezes were balmy and the sun was hot and love was supposed to last forever.

Bea watched him go. Something wild and wanton in her wanted to call out to him, to beg him to stay. But a sane, sensible part of her knew it was best to let him go. The sun caught in his hair, and it was so bright, she shaded her eyes, straining forward until all she could see of Russ was a distant shadow.

She imagined she heard the screen door shut behind him, although common sense told her the house was too far away for her to hear. She even imagined the sound of his footsteps on the stairs. He would be climbing upward now, going to get his duffle bag. It was not too late to stop him.

She half rose, then sank back down. There had been too many mistakes in her life, too many disappointments, too many heartbreaks. She wasn't about to compound the errors by going after a man whose future was uncertain at best, a man who had never professed any feelings at all for her except passion and a small bit of admiration.

She waited in the grove until he'd had time to leave; then she stood up and brushed the pine needles and clinging leaves off her clothes. Her face felt flushed. When she reached up, she felt the dampness on her cheeks. Lowering her hands, she inspected the moisture with surprise. Tears. She hadn't even realized she was crying.

She sniffed loudly and wiped her face. She had to be brave. She wasn't about to face Taylor with tears on her cheeks—even if they weren't tears for him.

Russ drove without thinking.

After saying goodbye to Bea's family, he left Florence and hit Highway 72, heading east toward Huntsville. He figured he might angle southward from there toward Birmingham, or maybe even southeast toward Atlanta. Usually he avoided the big cities, sticking to back roads and small towns. There was something soothing about small towns where he could smell the earth and feel the breezes from trees along the street and meander for miles and miles with never an interstate highway in sight. He supposed he was just a country boy at heart.

Someday, maybe, he'd buy another little place, maybe an orange grove in Florida or a cotton field in Georgia, or a soybean farm in Alabama. Someday... He let his thoughts trail off. No use thinking about someday. Best to think about right now.

Right now he thought he'd head to a big city. He needed a change of pace, something to make him forget a certain black-eyed woman.

The wind whistled around the truck's ill-fitting windows. His radio was dead, so he couldn't play country music. He drove with the sound of wind in his ears and the image of Bea in his mind. What was she doing now? Was she missing him?

There was a huge empty spot in the pit of his stomach, and he realized that he had never even finished his dinner. But he knew the ache had nothing to do with hunger. It had everything to do with a woman who smelled like spring and tasted like heaven.

He hoped her car was ready when she got back to Pearcy. He hoped she didn't have to depend on the kindness of another stranger to see her safely into Dallas.

Suddenly he knew he couldn't leave her, not yet, not until she was headed home to Dallas. He didn't want her to have to depend on strangers. Friends were so much nicer.

Ramming his foot on the brake, he pulled off at a small country store. The old truck rattled and squalled as he turned it around. Bea would be leaving Florence on Saturday, taking a rental car as far as Little Rock. From there she'd take a bus into Pearcy. He knew her plans, for she had told him early this morning.

The emptiness in his stomach vanished and he began whistling, tapping the rhythm on the steering wheel with his fingers. He was headed back to Paradise.

After Russ left, Bea went directly to her room, going up the back staircase in order to avoid questions. She didn't want to see anybody, especially not Taylor. She had too many things to think about.

The door to the guest bedroom was open. She didn't pause to look inside. Russ was no longer there. She could feel the emptiness wafting through the open doorway.

A fresh flood of tears gathered behind her eyelids and pushed their way down her cheeks. She had read somewhere that tears were good for you, but she'd be darned if she could comprehend how. Right now she felt as if she'd been wrung out by careless hands and left on the line, limp and damp, left there to flap around helplessly by herself.

She had never known the meaning of lonesome until today.

When she got to her bedroom, she locked the door. Then she sat in a chair beside her window, elbow on the windowsill, chin on her hands. How many times had she watched life from the window? How many times had she looked out that same window, hoping Taylor would come up the front walk? And now . . . She squeezed her eyes shut, but that didn't stop the thoughts. Now she was looking out the window hoping another man would come back, hoping and wishing and praying that Russ Hammond would come down the street in that truck so loud she could hear him a block away, come down the street and up the stairs and into her bedroom and whisk her off to never-never land where nobody ever left anybody behind.

Bea waited until the day she left Florence to face her father. He was staying at the local inn with his wife, Betsy. Bea asked to meet him in the dining room. She wanted neutral ground.

Taylor was already at the table when she arrived. He stood up, but made no move to touch her. She said a prayer of thanksgiving for that small favor.

"I'm glad you came, Bea."

"Don't be glad yet. I'm not here for a sentimental father-daughter reunion." She stood behind her chair, clutching it with tight fingers. The solid feel of the wood gave her something to cling to. "I have to know the truth, Taylor. I have to know why you left us, and why, during all those years, you never tried to see us. Not once."

"And you deserve to hear it. Sit down, Bea. We have a lot to talk about."

Taylor Adams told his daughter why he had left her. He explained about marriages that go bad, sometimes because of terrible things that two people do and say to each other, but most often because of neglect. He and Glory Ethel had neglected their marriage, and when Betsy came to town, he was ripe for a diversion, something to make him forget what he was missing at home. He had never meant to leave his family, never meant to divorce his wife. But Betsy became more than a diversion for him; she became his love, the greatest love of his life. And because he had been the one to stray, the marriage partner to go wrong, he had made a clean break, leaving Glory Ethel with full custody. At the time, it had seemed the best thing to do.

"It was a mistake, Bea, not coming back to see you and Samuel. I realize that now. I should have made amends with you years ago."

"It's a little too late for regrets, isn't it?"

"It's never too late. I've missed too many years of your life, and I can see how you must have believed that I never loved you. But I did, Bea. And I do. I swear that." He reached across the table, then, and took her hand. "I know I can't make the past up to you, but I want to be a part of your future."

"Are you absolutely certain this time?" She let her hand lie limp in his, not squeezing back, not giving him any reason to think that he could return and she'd let him into her life as if nothing had ever happened. "You have to be sure, Taylor. I don't think I could stand it if you left me twice."

"Oh, Bea." His anguish showed in the tight lines of his face and in his eyes, heavy with unshed tears. "I was so young and foolish. I never thought how you must have felt."

"It's still how I feel, Taylor. I can't change my feelings the way I change clothes, just shuck off the dirty and put on the clean."

"Let me try, Bea. Give me a second chance to be your father."

She considered his offer a long time before she spoke.

"What about Betsy?" she finally asked.

"She understands. She wants both of us to be a part of your life, if you'll let us."

"Hearts and flowers and fried chicken on Sunday? False smiles and make-believe hugs and let's pretend everything is wonderful?"

"No. All I'm asking is that we both take the time to know each other. I'm hoping the smiles and the hugs will be real, Bea. I'm hoping you'll learn to love me as I've always loved you."

At last Bea understood the hard choice her father had made and the courage it took for him to come to her after all these years—courage and love.

"I'm not making any promises, Taylor." She stood up, and when she smiled, it was the small, shy smile of a little girl trying to please her father. "But I'll try. I promise you that."

She leaned down and kissed him swiftly on the cheek. "Goodbye, Taylor."

He caught her hand. "For now, Bea."

She left him sitting in the restaurant with a smile on his face and tears in his eyes, and she hurried outside to her waiting rental car.

While Bea was making the transfer from rental car to bus in Little Rock, Arkansas, Russ was sitting in Room Two at the Paradise, wrestling with his private demons. He leaned against the headboard and stared at the black-and-white TV. The picture was meaningless and there was no sound, for he hadn't even bothered to turn up the volume.

"Her car is ready. There's no reason for me to stay." He spoke aloud, as if the sound of his own voice would convince him of the logic of leaving Pearcy.

"What I should do is get into my truck and head back to Florida. It's time to start over."

An actor on TV hung his head and cried. Russ felt like doing the same thing. What the devil was wrong with him?

"She doesn't need me anymore."

The actor on the screen was staring out the window now, huge tears rolling down his cheeks. Russ empathized. The thought of never seeing Bea Adams again filled him with such agony, he felt as if all life had been drained from his body. Not to hear her laughter, not to see her smile, not to touch her soft skin, not to taste her sweet lips—the pain was too much to bear.

"I should be going," he said aloud, even while he knew he would stay. And suddenly, sitting in a dingy motel room in Pearcy, Arkansas, he knew why he could never leave without seeing Bea. All his life he had wandered, not because he was running, but because he was searching, searching for a home. At last, he had found it.

Chapter Ten

It was late afternoon when the bus pulled into Pearcy, Arkansas. Bea was rumpled and tired. She smoothed the wrinkles from her skirt the best way she could and stepped down from the bus. The station was small and poorly lit. Dingy windows blocked what little sunshine there was, and one naked bulb cast a pale yellow glow over the plastic furniture and the faces of the weary travelers.

"Need any help, Tiger Lady?" Russ stepped from the shadows.

"Russ." Her hand flew to her throat. "I didn't expect to ever see you again."

"Neither did I." He took her elbow and led her to a row of plastic chairs. They sat down together, side by side, facing forward. It was the way they had traveled together, not touching, both looking off into the distance as if they were straining to see around the next bend.

She was acutely aware of him, his thigh barely brushing against the side of her skirt, the way his python boots looked against the dusty floor, the even tenor of his breathing, the sprinkling of hair along the backs of his hands. She held her breath, afraid to say anything lest he vanish, lest she find herself dreaming.

She held her breath so long she feared she might turn blue and faint. Finally he broke the long silence.

"When I left Florence, I thought I'd said goodbye to you, Bea." He turned to face her then. His eyes were as vivid as the bright blue ribbons used to tie bouquets sent to mothers of newborn boys—and just as eloquent.

She reached out and touched him, pressed her palm against his cheek and leaned forward, leaned so close she could see the sparkling centers of his eyes.

"I'm glad you couldn't say goodbye, Russ."

"Are you, Bea? Did you miss me?"

"Yes. I missed your smile. I missed your beard. I even missed your boots."

He laughed aloud. Several weary travelers paused on their way to the door to turn their heads and stare at him. Then, seeing nothing except a big man with a beard, they shook their heads and walked away.

"That's wonderful," he said. "Simply wonderful." He took her hands off his face and turned them palms up. Then he pressed them to his mouth, both at the same time. His breath was warm on her skin, and his kiss was sweet. "I'm can't believe it."

"Why?"

"I don't remember anybody ever missing me, Bea. It feels so good."

He kissed her hands again, and they studied each other for another long while.

Now that he had come all the way to Pearcy, now that she was actually here, Russ was having a hard time knowing what to say. He'd never wanted anything in his life as much as he wanted Bea Adams. And yet, even in the dusty bus station, she seemed as remote and unattainable as an expensive porcelain doll sitting on the highest shelf of the most exclusive store in town. He'd learned early not to ask for things he couldn't have, and the habit seemed to be with him still.

What if he said the wrong thing? What if she didn't want him? He squeezed her hands, agonizing over his choice of words.

She saved him.

"What are you doing in Pearcy, Arkansas?"

"I came back to be sure your car was ready to travel."

"Is it?"

"Yes."

"I couldn't stand the thought of you having to ask a stranger for help."

"That was kind of you."

"Maybe it was selfish. I didn't like to think of you stuck on a mountain with another man."

They both remembered their time on the mountain. It seemed so long ago.

Russ released her hands and cleared his throat.

"I wasn't going to see you again, Bea. I was going to check on your car and leave."

"And go where, Russ? California? Texas? Wyoming?"

"Florida." She drew in a quick breath. "I'm going back to LaBelle, Florida. I'm going to get another grove, Bea. Start all over."

"I'm glad."

A silence fell on them again. Bea thought of Florida. It seemed such a long way from Dallas.

"Come with me, Bea," Russ said suddenly, startling both of them. Once he'd said the words, he felt bolder. "Come to Florida with me."

"I'm on my way back to Dallas. I have to be back at work on Wednesday. I can't extend my vacation any longer than that."

"I'm not dead set on Florida, Bea. If you don't like Florida, I could live in Texas or Alabama just as well."

"I just got back from a vacation in Alabama, Russ." She chose her words carefully, not wanting to hope for things he wasn't offering. "If this is an invitation to come and visit you, I'll be happy to visit wherever you go. Just let me know when you get settled."

"I'm not talking about an extended vacation or an invitation to visit."

Her blood roared in her ears and her heart climbed up into her throat. She sat very still, not trusting herself to speak.

"I'm talking about marriage, Bea." Russ took her left hand between his. "I never dreamed it would be like this. I never thought I'd find somebody to love. And I certainly never pictured myself proposing in a dingy bus station in Pearcy, Arkansas."

"You're asking me to marry you?"

"Does it shock you that much, Bea?"

She thought about their journey together—the night in the tent on Quachita Mountain, the hours in his truck cab, closed off from the rest of the world by the storm, the meeting in the grove behind her house. Her trip had been more than an odyssey home: it had been an odyssey to love.

"No," she whispered. "I'm not shocked."

"I don't know when I started loving you." Russ caught her hand again and held it tightly. "Maybe it was the minute I saw you on that mountain road pretending you knew how to fix your car."

"I think it was those python boots that did me in."

They smiled into each other's eyes.

"At first I didn't even recognize it," he said. "I was sitting on a sagging bed at the Paradise, telling myself I needed to get into my truck and head south to Florida when I knew that I couldn't go without you." He squeezed her hand. "I love you. Do you love me, Bea?"

"Yes. God knows, I didn't want to." She pressed one hand against his cheek. "I guess love is one of those things we can't plan." She smiled at him then, a smile of such radiance he thought the sun had suddenly risen behind her chair. "By the time we got to Florence, I suspected it. But when you left me in the grove, I knew it. I love you, Russ."

"Will you marry me?"

She studied his face as the thought of marriage and all its complications played through her mind.

"Can't we have love without marriage, Russ? Can't we visit each other, be with each other without taking that kind of step?"

"We could, Bea, but I don't want to. I don't want to be lonesome in Florida while you're lonesome in Dallas. I don't want to lie in an empty bed and wish you were there."

He grew silent, turning his head and looking out across the nearly empty bus station; but he didn't seem to be seeing the cobwebs and the dust and the stiff plastic chairs. He was looking at something Bea couldn't see.

"I don't pledge my love lightly, Bea. You're the first person I've ever really loved—except my parents, and I hardly remember them. This is not a letting-go kind of love; this is not the kind of thing I shared with Lurlene. If you marry me, it will be forever. You will be my home and I will be yours—till death do us part."

If Bea had any doubts about marrying Russ, they all vanished, swept away by the tide of his abiding love. She was on the verge of telling him yes when he stood up.

His chair rattled and threatened to tip over. He steadied it with his hand.

For a moment, he towered over her, gazing down at the top of her head. Then suddenly he was on his knees in front of her, reaching for her hand.

"Russ." She laughed. "What in the world are you doing?"

"This is an old-fashioned proposal, Bea. I wish I had moonlight and soft music and wine, but I guess all this grandeur will have to do." His eyes swept around the bus station, taking in the cobwebs on the ceiling, the tacky plastic chairs, the dingy walls and their peeling yellow paint, the dusty floors.

"I want you to be my wife. I want to love you and cherish you and protect you for now and forever. I want you to wear my ring and bear my children. I want to wake up in the morning with you at my side. I want your face to be the last thing I see before I go to sleep each night."

Love shone in his eyes, as bright and vivid as a summer day, and Bea knew it was a forever kind of love.

"Say yes, Bea."

"Yes, Russ." She bent down and pressed her cheek against his. "Oh, yes." He felt the dampness of her tears.

He leaned back and tenderly wiped her cheeks. "Don't cry, Tiger Lady. This is a time of happy celebration."

"I'm not crying because I'm sad, I'm crying because I almost lost you."

"You can never lose me. I promise you that."

They kissed then, and it was like coming home.

Afterward, Russ gathered her bags and escorted her to his pickup. When they were inside the cab, they grinned at each other for a while, pleased with themselves and the world.

"I guess you'll want a big wedding in Florence with all your family?"

That was exactly what Bea had been thinking, but when Russ asked her, he looked so lonesome, she couldn't bear the thought of waiting all the months it would take to plan a big family wedding.

"Let's get married here, Russ."

"Here?"

"Right here in the mountains where we found each other. Just the two of us. We can have a big celebration with my family later."

He pulled her into his arms for a heart-to-heart hug.

"You know why I've been loving you so long?" he asked, leaning his cheek against her soft hair. "Because you make me feel special."

"That's what I was thinking about you."

He leaned back to look at her. "When?"

"Always."

That called for another kiss, and another, and another, until the windows were so fogged he had to wipe them with his handkerchief so he could see to drive. Then they went to Freddy's General Store for a private celebration dinner.

Freddy joined in the festivities by spreading a piece of oilcloth on the cracker barrel and decorating the makeshift table with a birthday candle stuffed into a beer bottle. He served his specialty, fried catfish and hushpuppies. Bea and Russ declared it was the best meal they'd ever had, and they meant it.

"Now I've got a special treat for the bride-to-be," Freddy said. He disappeared behind a counter piled high with yard goods, assorted cheese cut in hunks and wrapped with plastic, spools of thread in every color of the rainbow, and a few selected brands of chewing tobacco. When he emerged, he was holding high a Cracker Jack box.

"Dessert." Freddy put the box on the table with a flourish.

Laughing, Bea and Russ opened the box and began to feed each other the caramel-coated popcorn. They ate to the bottom of the box, with Freddy standing by grinning. When they had finished eating, Russ started to crumple the box.

"Wait," Freddy said. "You missed something."

Russ reached into the box and pulled out a small plastic-wrapped trinket.

"I forgot about the prize," he said, tearing off the wrapper. A make-believe engagement ring lay in the palm of his hand, its glass "diamond" winking in the light of the candle.

He got down on his knees and took Bea's left hand in his.

"Every woman should have an engagement ring." He slipped the ring solemnly on her finger.

"Every woman should have a man like you." She leaned over and kissed the top of his head.

He closed her left hand into a small fist and clasped it between his hands. Then he smiled up at her.

"Bea, this will have to do until I can buy you the real thing."

"This is the real thing, a gift of love. What more could a woman want?"

Russ laughed and looked up at Freddy.

"I think I'll marry this woman," he joked. "Do you know where I can find a justice of the peace?"

"You're looking at him." Freddy chuckled. "In a town like Pearcy, a man has to wear many hats. I also fill in for the barber, in case you want a haircut . . . or that beard shaved off."

"Don't you dare." Bea cupped Russ's face. "I don't want a hair on his head changed."

They all laughed and took turns admiring Bea's ring. Freddy brought out a bottle of his favorite wine, muscadine, made in his kitchen using his secret recipe. Bea and Russ declared it was the best wine they'd ever had. They meant that, too.

Finally, warmed by laughter and love and wine, they made their way back to the Paradise. Sitting in the truck, holding hands, they looked at the neon sign blinking orange and green. Both of them were thinking of all the sign promised.

"I have a room," Russ said.

"I guessed you might." Her hand tightened on his.

"I want you there."

"I do, too."

"More than anything, Bea."

"I know."

Suddenly he pulled her into his arms and gathered her close to his heart. She laced her arms around his neck and buried her fingers in his thick hair.

"Bea." His voice was muffled against her cheek.

"Hmm?" Hers was smothered in his neck.

"Would you mind terribly if we waited? I know it seems pointless and old-fashioned, but I want everything about our marriage to be perfect. I want us to start our life together as husband and wife in a marriage bed that will be sacred."

"Russ . . ." She could hardly speak for tears welling in her throat. "You are the sweetest, most wonderful man in the world. For you, I'd wait forever."

"It will just be a few days, until we get the blood tests and license."

They got Bea a separate room, and then Russ stayed with her until the wee hours of the morning, talking, planning, touching, but most of all, belonging to someone.

They were married in Pearcy at the back of Freddy's General Store. He had decorated it for the occasion. Pine boughs and Christmas tinsel were strung around the ceiling. Two life-size angels, borrowed from the Baptist church's Nativity set, stood guard beside the potbellied stove. Twenty-five birthday candles, assorted colors, stuck in brown beer bottles were lit and glowing on the counter.

Bea wore a yellow wool business suit and carried a bouquet of autumn leaves.

Freddy's wife, Miss Honey June, stood up as witness, wearing her best girdle and her Sunday hat with the artificial roses. Her sister, who usually stood up with her, was in bed with flu; so the local sheriff had been pulled in to witness. In deference to the occasion, he wore a plastic lily of the valley in his gun holster. The gun was hidden in his boot.

Russ and Bea pledged their vows and then stayed for a brief reception, hosted by Freddy and Miss Honey June. Everybody in town came, including the cats and dogs. The men bore Russ off to give him some friendly advice, and the women took charge of Bea.

Usually she didn't like being taken charge of, but the women were so cute and gave such funny advice, such as feed your man redeye gravy if you want boys, that she had a wonderful time.

After the reception, they honeymooned at the Paradise. Russ carried his bride over the threshold of Room Two and kicked the door shut behind them.

"Do you know how much I wanted you that night I came to this room with wine and cheese?" he asked.

"Do you know how much I wanted you to want me?"

"It didn't show."

She wrapped her arms around his neck and pulled his face close to hers. "Does it show now?"

"You'll have to convince me, Mrs. Hammond."

She traced his lips with her tongue, then left a damp trail down the side of his neck.

"Hmmmm. That's a start." He lowered her to the bed and poised himself over her. "Show me more."

She reached for his shirt buttons. "Do you mind if I start with that magnificent chest, Mr. Hammond?"

"You start with mine, I'll start with yours." He peeled his shirt off and began to unbutton her blouse.

She closed her eyes, letting the heat of his fingers warm her. She felt the last button pop open, felt him tugging her blouse from her waistband.

With her silk blouse and yellow jacket open like a flower on the bed, Russ bent over her. He traced her eyes, her cheeks, her mouth, then let his fingers trail down the side of her neck. Blood rushed to the surface of her skin, and she felt warm and tingly.

"I want to please you in every way, Bea."

"You please me, Russ." She laced her hands around his neck and pulled him down to her. "You please me very much."

"Bea . . . I can't believe you're mine."

Wrapping her close in his embrace, he captured her lips. With exquisite tenderness, he showed her what love meant to him; he showed her that she was his wife, his love, his hearth, his home.

And she responded in kind. Her kiss told him that his search was over, her fears were behind her and that, together, they would build a future, a haven safe from the storms that would sometimes buffet their lives.

The kiss seemed to endure forever, but they had all the time in the world. They had a lifetime.

After a long while, Russ lifted his head and gazed into her face.

"Do you have any idea what you mean to me, Bea?"

"I want to hear you say the words, Russ. They are precious to me."

"You mean more to me than a fireplace in the snow, more than orange groves in the sunshine. . . ." His face alight with the special glow of one who loves deeply and truly, Russ tenderly traced her cheekbone. "You mean more to me than life itself."

She reached for him, and they came together, his lips on hers. They savored each other, slowly, deliciously. And then his hands began to move over her body, raking aside clothing as it hampered his exploration. And when she lay beneath him, satin-skinned and splendid, he rose up and shed his clothes.

The beauty of him took her breath away. She lifted her hands to his chest, burying them in the golden hair covering the muscular exposure.

"I never knew a man could be so beautiful."

"Touch me, Bea."

He lay beside her once more, and they learned each other, wondering at the miracle that had befallen them. Neither of them had set out to find love, but somehow it had found them. They would never cease to wonder at that miracle.

The slow, sweet exploration gathered speed and intensity until finally, they were straining toward each other, their breaths raspy and their skin tingling with the heat of passion. They wanted more. They wanted heart against heart, flesh against flesh. But they also wanted to savor the moment, to draw out the anticipation, to tease and tantalize until neither could stand it any longer.

The moment came sooner than they had expected. She was against the pillows and he was poised above her.

"Bea?"

"Oh, yes, my love. Yes."

They became one then, their bodies joining as surely as their hearts had already joined. The wonder and the beauty and the love of a sacred marriage was theirs in their tiny motel room in the Paradise.

When they found release, they lay together, their heads side by side on the pillows, their fingers entwined. A tiny swatch of sunshine slated through a crack in the curtains, striking sparks in Russ's blond hair. It gave him a halo.

Bea lifted herself on her elbow to look at him.

"My guardian angel," she whispered.

"Always, Bea . . . Always."

They decided to drive both their vehicles down to Hot Springs and trade them in for one.

"This is is a brand-new start for us," Russ told Bea as they stood outside the Paradise the morning after their wedding. "I want us to travel in something that will reflect the solidity of this marriage."

"I mainly want us to travel together."

"Well said, Mrs. H."

Russ kissed her soundly, then helped her into her Jaguar. He led off and she followed, and when they got to a car dealership in Hot Springs, they decided on a sturdy, plain station wagon.

"It looks as if it will go for miles and never break down," Bea said.

"I was thinking of the children," Russ said.

"Children?" Her face got pink.

"Yes. It's big enough for a large family. You do want children, don't you?"

He was so anxious looking, she had to laugh.

"Only about six."

"For a minute there, you had me fooled, Bea Hammond."

Russ loved her new name and took every opportunity to say it.

"If you think I'm going to sit in a stuffy office while you're having fun romping in the orange groves with the children, you're sadly mistaken, Mr. Hammond. I want my children to know who their mother is."

They kissed, heedless of the stares and smiles of the car salesman, and then they signed papers and trans-

ferred ownership and drove south toward Dallas in their
brand-new station wagon. They had decided they would
go there first in order for Bea to settle her affairs.

Russ had talked of flying on to Florida to get a head
start on finding a citrus grove and a place to stay, but he
hadn't talked with any great enthusiasm about it. The
plain fact was, he didn't want to leave Bea. Now that he
had found her, he didn't want to ever leave her, not even
for a few days.

That suited Bea fine. She didn't want him to leave,
either.

"We'll find our home together," she had told him.

He'd kissed her and said that she was his home. She
kissed him right back and said that he was hers. They
both said that love was remarkable and marriage was
heaven.

Finally, they left Hot Springs in their new station
wagon, sitting side by side, Russ driving with one hand
and holding Bea's with the other. He looked out the
window most of the time, and she spent all her time
looking at him and marveling.

They stopped for lunch at a picnic spot in southwest
Arkansas.

While Russ spread out the lunch, Bea went to the
bathroom. Like many bathrooms in remote places, it
was dark and dingy. She groped her way through the
semigloom. Out of the dark came sounds. Bea jumped;
then she investigated.

In a far corner of the bathroom, huddled under the
sink were two mongrel puppies, their hair matted and
their skin stretched over jutting bones.

"Oh, you poor darlings." She bent over them, pet-
ting and soothing both at the same time. "Whose puppies are you? Where did you come from?"

They snuffled and sniffled, and when Bea stood up, they followed her. Every step she took, they took, too.

"Poor little waifs. Poor little orphans."

She gathered them up in her arms and carried them outside to Russ.

"Guess what, darling?"

He turned and saw the squirming bundle in her arms.

"What do you have, Bea?"

"I've already made you a father." She came close and handed him one of the puppies. "From me to you with love. Aren't they precious?"

"With a little tender loving care, they will be."

Bea thought he was nearly as happy over the puppies as he had been over their wedding. She was glad. He had given her a glass diamond and she had given him stray puppies, but both had been gifts straight from the heart. And they were the very best kind.

The puppies ate most of the lunch, with Bea and Russ watching and laughing. Then the four of them loaded into the station wagon and set out for Dallas. They stopped at the nearest store and purchased puppy food, two plastic bowls and two small collars.

"I'll take them to the vet as soon as we're in Dallas," he said.

Since most motels refused to let puppies into the room, Bea and Russ found a camping spot and he set up the tent.

That night Bea got to find out what it was like to sleep in Russ's sleeping bag. He tucked her in with tender care, the way one would tuck a child in at day's end, and then he crawled in beside her. Snug against him, with the bag making a warm cocoon around them, she felt more cherished than she'd ever felt in her life.

She loved the way they fit together, just right, and the way his beard tickled her, and the way his voice became musical when he murmured words of love to her. A storm began to brew outside their tent, but she never even noticed. Russ was her focus, the center of her universe, and for a while, nothing existed for her except him.

And at last, when he had placed her head on his shoulder and she could hear the even sound of his breathing, she fell asleep.

It rained and rained during the night. Thunder crashed and lightning flashed, but Bea slept on, safe and secure in Russ's arms.

When they woke up the next morning, their new station wagon was mired in the mud so deep they couldn't move it, either forward or backward. Since they were the only people at the campground, the two of them set to work to free the station wagon.

"Try it again, Bea!" Russ yelled. She was in the driver's seat and he was behind, pushing.

She stomped down on the accelerator. The tires spun, slinging mud onto his boots and the legs of his jeans.

"I think it's hopeless, Russ," she called.

"Nothing's hopeless, Bea. Not since I married you."

He gathered pine boughs to make a ramp for the sunken tires, and soon the station wagon was out of the mire and onto firmer ground. Together they started loading their camping gear.

"You should see your face, Russ. Mud all over."

"Where?"

"Here. And here. And here." She showed him all the places, standing with her legs planted between his, and soon they got sidetracked.

"Hmm," he said as he kissed her. "Now you should see yours."

The situation called for a bath, so they took their towels to a secluded stream in the woods and bathed. They got sidetracked again, and by the time they came out of the stream, clean and shining and happy, it was time to eat lunch.

They whistled and called their two new puppies, Pearcy and Florence, named for the places that had brought them together. The puppies were nowhere in sight.

"Poor little tykes," Russ said. "I guess all that commotion getting the car out of the mud scared them."

"I thought they were asleep in the tent."

"I did, too."

Hand in hand, Bea and Russ searched for their lost pets. Within twenty minutes, they had found them. Both puppies sat at attention on their skinny haunches, their sharp little teeth bared and their ears stiff with excitement.

"What in the world is going on?" Bea said. "Florence, come here."

Florence grandly ignored her. So did Pearcy. They growled to show their fierceness, and kept their vigil at a small redbud tree.

"I think I see the problem." Russ went to the tree and reached into the branches. He came out with a bedraggled kitten. "Who has left you behind, little fellow?"

The kitten studied him with eyes that looked too big in his scrawny face, then he turned on his motor and began to purr so loudly, Russ and Bea laughed.

"That's a big sound for such a small cat," Bea said.

"What do you expect from the Hammond pets? We have nothing but the biggest and the best." Russ smoothed the kitten's damp, tangled fur. The purring got louder. "Bea, I think Dallas likes me. In fact, I may be his favorite person in the whole world."

"I wouldn't doubt that a minute. You're *my* favorite person in the whole world."

Soon the five of them were on their way once more to Dallas. Russ was driving with Pearcy curled up next to his leg, snoring and dreaming of chasing rabbits. Florence was crumpled on top of Bea's feet, twitching her ears and thinking of pimento sandwiches. And little Dallas was perched on Bea's shoulder, looking back the way they had come and thanking her lucky stars she'd found these new people, especially the big one with the tickly beard. Bea was smiling so widely she thought she must look foolish. But she didn't care. She had Russ and three fine pets. What more could a woman want?

They arrived in Dallas without further misadventure, and spent a week there setting Bea's affairs in order. She would run the business from where she and Russ finally settled, but for now she delegated the work to trusted professionals. She took only her personal things with her—her clothes, an album of family pictures and her favorite books.

"Are you sure this is all you want to take, Bea?"

Her belongings were piled on the sidewalk, three suitcases, two boxes and her briefcase. She hadn't realized until she saw them spread out that way how little she had that was important to her. It was as if she had purposely kept her life bare of treasured possessions for fear they would somehow vanish.

"You remember when we used to say how different we were, Russ?"

"It seems so long ago."

"I don't think we were so different, after all. Everything I have that's important to me, I can fit in the back seat of the car."

"I believe I'm too big for the trunk, Bea. And how about Florence and Pearcy and Dallas? They might smother."

She buried her hands in his beard and pulled his face close enough to kiss.

"I'm not talking about you, you big wonderful rambling man. I'm talking about *things*."

"*Things?* Who needs them?"

They set out for Florida on a bright sunshiny day, with the colors of autumn celebrating their odyssey. Their three pets were on the second seat, fatter now and content and not at all fearful of being abandoned, sleeping cuddled together in a tight ball so that it was hard to tell where one left off and the other began. Bea sat snuggled close to Russ, listening to him hum along to an old country ballad on the radio.

A month ago, she would never have dreamed that she could love country music. Or that she would be sleeping through thunderstorms. Of course, she told herself, that didn't mean she was changing completely. She would always be her own woman, sharing herself with Russ, but independent in some ways, still. And she would never, *never* fly. She could guarantee that. Almost.

They camped all the way to Florida, with the sun shining down on every mile of road, and Dallas and Florence and Pearcy behaving like angels. *Mischievous* angels.

And when they arrived in LaBelle, Florida, where the sky was so blue it hurt their eyes and the cabbage trees swayed in the breeze and the Caloosahatchee River meandered lazily alongside Highway 80 and the air was sweet with the smell of citrus blossoms, Bea and Russ knew that they had come home.

He drove her through the small town, pointing out the historic Henry County Courthouse and the corner grocery and the big white Baptist church. They stopped long enough for gas and refreshments; then Russ headed out of town, northwest, toward the groves.

Citrus groves dotted the land like confetti. Row after row of fruit trees marched alongside the road in strict formation. Bea pressed her face to the window, for she knew she was seeing more than citrus groves. She was seeing her future.

Russ turned onto a gravel road and parked between a row of lemon trees. Yellow-and-green fruit hung from the branches, and the air was sharp and sweet with the smell of ripening citrus.

Russ helped Bea from the car and stood with his arm around her waist.

"Bea, I want you to see what a citrus grove looks like. I want you to touch the leaves, to smell the fruit, to feel the rich earth underneath your feet."

She reached out and caught a waxy green leaf between her fingers. Even after she plucked it off she could still feel the flow of life through the tiny leaf.

"It gets awfully hot down here, and we don't have any winter to speak of. Sometimes you think the mosquitoes are going to carry you off, and you might get sick of the sweet smell of citrus."

He paused, looking out across the grove. Then he turned back to her.

"There will be bad years when the crops will be diseased or when an unexpected freeze destroys crops and trees alike. It won't be an easy living, Bea. I'll have to buy a grove, get established in the business all over again. In fact, there will be some lean times."

"Are you trying to talk me out of living in Florida?" She smiled at him.

"No. I just want you to know what it will be like. If you have any doubts, tell me now and we'll go somewhere else." He tipped her face up with his index finger. "I'm willing to live anywhere, Bea, as long as you're there."

"You love it down here, don't you, Russ?"

"One of the best times of my life was when I walked through my groves and felt a piece of earth beneath my feet and knew it was mine." He circled his thumb on her chin. "Yes, Bea. I love it."

"Then, Russ Hammond, here I am, and here I will stay."

"Welcome home, Bea Hammond." He leaned down to claim her lips. "Now and forever."

Epilogue

The family was celebrating the tenth wedding anniversary of Glory Ethel and Jedidiah. They had all gathered in Florida, at the home of Russ and Bea Hammond, and now they were spread out on the lawn, playing a lively game of Red Rover.

"Red Rover, Red Rover, send Grandma right over." The speaker was Glory Hammond, and she was seven years old. Her clear, childish voice rang out like church bells, and her bright blond hair sparkled in the sunlight. Everybody said she was a chip off the old block, her daddy's block.

Little Miss Glory Hammond squeezed the hand of her six-year-old brother, Rusty, and he darted his black eyes her way.

"Don't yell so loud. Grandma's not deef."

"The word is *deaf*, Mr. Smarty." Glory, who was never accused of being without spunk, stuck out her tongue at her brother.

"Children." Laughing, Bea shifted Baby Laurel on her hips. "Don't quarrel."

"I'm not a squirrel." Rusty's dark hair stood up in a cowlick as he turned toward a higher authority. "Daddy, I'm not a squirrel, am I?"

"Not very often." Russ stifled his laughter. "Mother means don't fight with your sister."

"Okay." Rusty, ever the cheerful peacemaker, turned his attention back to the game. "Hey, Grandma. Are you comin' or not?"

"I'm coming, Rusty." Glory Ethel hiked her skirts up almost to her knees.

Jedidiah whistled. She gave him a flirty wink.

"Not now, you old Romeo." She started across the lawn at a respectable trot, her gray hair flying around her smiling face.

"Mother, be careful." Samuel Adams was the one who issued the warning. He was sitting in a swing under a tree with his wife, watching his beautiful blond eight-year-old daughter and his two five-year-old twin sons with a fierce paternal pride.

Molly, sitting by his side, huge in the third trimester of her pregnancy, smiled lovingly at him. He was more relaxed now than he'd ever been, but from time to time, he still assumed his role as keeper of the family. That was all right by her. She loved him in all his roles.

Everybody watched as Glory Ethel put on her final burst of speed and tried to break through the joined hands of her grandchildren. She couldn't, of course, and of all her grandchildren, only her namesake, Little Miss Glory, suspected that she wasn't trying very hard.

"Dear me," Glory Ethel said. "You children have won again."

"That's 'cause you so old, Grandma," Rusty said.

The game broke up amid general laughter. Samuel and Molly collected their brood, bid their goodbyes and headed to their hotel. Glory Ethel and Jedidiah proclaimed that their great old age demanded an afternoon nap.

"I'll bet some other little people I know could use a nap," Glory Ethel said as she took Rusty and Glory by the hand and led them into the sprawling white house.

"Come here, little one." Jedidiah took Baby Laurel and followed them. He turned and winked over his shoulder at Russ and Bea. "I was young once, too."

Holding the tiniest Hammond carefully, Jedidiah walked toward the house, still spry and upright. Pearcy and Florence trotted along behind, wagging their tails; and Dallas stalked up the rear, pretending he was a lion guarding his pride.

Bea and Russ watched until their family was safely inside the house, then they joined hands and headed to the citrus grove. Their laughter floated in the clear air, mingling with the fragrance of orange blossoms. Underneath their feet, fallen petals sprinkled the earth like drops of sugar frosting.

Russ led Bea deep into the grove, faraway from the house. It was their special private place, one they'd come to many times during the eight years of their marriage. And it was as fresh to them as the first time they'd ever come there together.

Russ stood under an orange tree in full blossom and drew his wife into his arms. Tipping her chin up with the back of his hand, he looked into her eyes.

"Mrs. Hammond. Have I told you lately that I love you?"

She pretended to be in deep thought. "Let's see . . .

once this morning. No, twice. Then again after lunch, and once during the game of Red Rover, I think." She was smiling with her eyes crinkled at the corners. "That makes four, I believe."

"You're counting?" He pretended outrage.

"Absolutely. That's the only way to keep you on your toes."

He nuzzled her neck, inhaling the mingled fragrances of her skin and the orange blossoms falling on her dark hair.

"Mrs. Hammond...this is serious, now. Stop chuckling." He lifted his head and tried to look serious. He failed. His mouth tipped up at the corners and his blue eyes danced with merriment. "Have I *shown* you lately that I love you?"

She shook her head, mock serious. "It seems forever."

"We'll have to remedy that."

And he did. He pulled her down where the orange blossoms lay scattered on the fertile earth, and they pledged their love once more and forever.

* * * * *

WRITTEN IN THE STARS

Travel along with
THE MAN FROM NATCHEZ
by Elizabeth August

When a lovely lady waves a red flag to tempt the Taurus man, will the bullheaded hunk charge into romance... or be as stubborn as ever? Find out in May in THE MAN FROM NATCHEZ by Elizabeth August... the fifth book in our Written in the Stars series!

Rough and rugged farmer Nate Hathaway wasn't about to let Stacy Jamison go it alone while searching for treasure in the Shenandoah Mountains! The man from Natchez was about to embark on a very tempting trip....

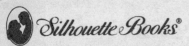

IT'S A CELEBRATION OF MOTHERHOOD!

Following the success of BIRDS, BEES and BABIES, we are proud to announce our second collection of Mother's Day stories.

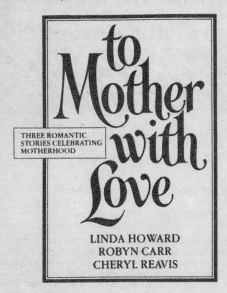

to
Mother
with
Love

THREE ROMANTIC
STORIES CELEBRATING
MOTHERHOOD

LINDA HOWARD
ROBYN CARR
CHERYL REAVIS

Three stories in one volume, all by award-winning authors—stories especially selected to reflect the love all families share.

Available in May, TO MOTHER WITH LOVE is a perfect gift for yourself or a loved one to celebrate the joy of motherhood.

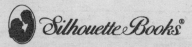 *Silhouette Books*®